THE ORPHANS

Other books by Berniece Rabe

The Girl Who Had No Name
Naomi
Rass

THE ORPHANS

Berniece Rabe

E. P. Dutton   New York

Library of Congress Cataloging in Publication Data

Rabe, Berniece.   The orphans.

SUMMARY: An orphaned twin brother and sister living
in rural Missouri during the Depression finally find a
permanent home.
[1. Orphans—Fiction.   2. Twins—Fiction.
3. Country life—Fiction]   I. Title.
PZ7.R105Or   1978   [Fic]   78-9418   ISBN 0-525-36450-1

Published in the United States by E. P. Dutton, a Division
of Sequoia-Elsevier Publishing Company, Inc., New York

Published simultaneously in Canada by Clarke,
Irwin & Company Limited, Toronto and Vancouver
Editor: Ann Durell   Designer: Jennifer Dossin

Printed in the U.S.A.   First Edition
10 9 8 7 6 5 4 3 2 1

For my grandchildren
Rochelle, Justin and Jeremy Rabe

one

Little Adam's stomach was full to bursting. Still, he felt drawn back to the long table spread in the front yard of G-Mama's little cabin. The cabin was also filled to bursting as it nestled there in the woods like a setting hen spreading an aura of love and caring over all the family. It was a right good pleasure to soak up the warmth of the day and the warmth of his family clustered around him.

Even the bugs had gathered for their share of the feast. Little Adam had been assigned to shoo them off the table but he didn't shoo very hard. He figured they had to eat too. It didn't matter, like it didn't matter that Uncle Windy and Uncle Burl were late getting back from town with the chunk of ice to make ice water.

Everybody had just gone ahead, once they got

1

tired of waiting, and had begun to eat their fill of greens, fried chicken, boiled potatoes, and yellow cake and raisin pies. No one complained about wanting a cold drink, for this was a day of kinfolk saying happy words and smiling away the sweat and worry of regular living.

It was a time to know you belonged in a family; know that you had two uncles, two aunts, a G-Mama, lots of big cousins, and a twin all your own even if you only saw her at gatherings like this. It was a time to know there was food aplenty for everybody.

There was gobs of leftovers on the table right now, sitting there waiting for his uncles. If he cared to, he could go back and fill his plate twenty or thirty times, or even a hundred, maybe, and it wouldn't be missed. Little Adam tested his belt to see if he had room in his stomach for one more helping of jelly-filled cake, and then took it. The cake crumbled dry in his mouth, like the day, and would have gone down a little better with the help of a tall glass of ice water.

But who minded how hot and dry the day was? Who minded that the green leaves on the trees were crackling brittle in their dust coverings? This was reunion time at G-Mama's and it was good. It was the time that Uncle Windy and Uncle Burl collected their children and came to pay their respects to G-Mama, the woman who had been their mother most of their lives. Just about any minute Uncle Windy would come sailing around the corner in a cloud of dust and the feasting could begin all over again.

It didn't surprise Adam that a billow of dust rose above the road and a truck came to a screeching halt no sooner than the thought had left his mind. But that wasn't Uncle Windy's red Ford. That truck was old and black, and Sheriff Erica Wheeler materialized out of the dust to demand, "G-Mama Braggs here? Run and get her, would you, sonny?"

Adam didn't move. Two of his big cousins who could run faster than he, and who were closer to the house, had heard the request. They were practically inside already, screaming for G-Mama to come out. Adam preferred to stand still and study the face of this woman sheriff. Something was wrong, for the face held a closed blank look that grown-ups often use when they don't want kids to know what their business is. It was law business she was hiding, no doubt.

Little Adam and Eva had been left orphans in 1932, and Uncle Windy and Uncle Burl were zooming over to lay claim on them when they ran into a roadblock and trouble with Sheriff Erica Wheeler. But that was seven years ago come Christmas. And that was too long for a sheriff to carry a grudge against Uncle Windy for finding a loophole in the law and getting himself straight out of trouble. Still, if she was a woman like Aunt Viv, she could carry a grudge for a long time.

3

"Did you arrest my Uncle Windy?" he demanded of the sheriff.

"It's against the law to talk like that to the law," Eva, his twin, whispered.

Adam didn't look towards his sister nor acknowledge her warning. "You got him locked up?"

The sheriff started to say something, but she got hold on herself and put that blank don't-mess-in-my-business look back on her face. So Adam kept right on talking.

"You had no claim on them that time they outrun you. That sign clearly stated that the five-hundred dollar fine or two years in prison was for tampering with the lock on the detour gate. The sign didn't say nothing at all about it being against the law to pull up the gateposts and go on through. My Uncle Windy never has disobeyed the law. You got no right locking him up."

At first Erica Wheeler acted like she might let his words just ride on by her in a sort of left-handed way. Then she glanced at him directly for a second, adjusted the band of her corduroy skirt until the center seam rested dead center and her gun fell at a natural hand level. She cleared her throat three times.

Then in a voice too nice to match any of the rough and toughness that Uncle Windy always credited her with, she said, "I'll bet you're that son of Adam Braggs, the boy Windy's been raising. Your Uncle Windy didn't break any law, Burl was driving. Look now, you take this little girl and . . ."

4

"That's my sister, Eva. We'll wait. G-Mama is coming."

G-Mama was so small that her apron almost wrapped around her twice but her voice was big and happy as she called out, "Ericky, you don't need come around checking on me when I got my whole family here visiting. What can I do for you?"

Erica Wheeler looked around at all the people that were gathering and seemed lost for words again, but only for a second. "I'm sorry, G-Mama. It's part of my job. I hate to bring you the news, but your boys are gone."

"Gone where? They was just goin' . . ." G-Mama stopped. "Ericky, don't! My boys ain't dead!"

Wails went up from the two aunts and the cousins, and Erica Wheeler had her arms stretched out supporting G-Mama, allowing her to beat away at her in her anguish.

Adam couldn't think. He just plain couldn't think. He reached his hand over to clasp the hand of his sister. Eva cried out, "Little Adam, we're orphans again!"

Adam didn't answer. For a minute he backed his thinking back to the place where he'd thought his Uncle Windy had been arrested. He let his mind set on that and pretend that that was why the sheriff had come and why the women were crying out. Sheriff Erica Wheeler wasn't crying; she was standing strong and stable talking to G-Mama.

Eva finally stopped her sobbing and let go of his

hand. "Didn't you hear, Little Adam? The sheriff says our uncles are dead. They was hit by a train!"

"I heard," said Adam.

"Something is the matter with you, Little Adam. You ain't crying. Why ain't you crying? We're twins, and you ought to cry same as me when you hurt."

"Maybe I ain't like you all the time, Eva. I guess I'll go out to the cow shed. I guess I won't stay out here anymore." But first he wanted to say something to the sheriff. "Ma'am, I guess I yelled at you, but . . . well, you see, I didn't ever think my Uncle Windy would be dead and . . ."

Sheriff Erica Wheeler looked straight at him as if he weren't just a ten-year-old kid and said, "Don't have to apologize to me or anyone for being on the side of your uncle. Don't ever stop feeling that way towards him. He was a good man."

He took her words and went on along to the cow shed and sat there in the empty stall for an hour or more thinking on them. The cow was out roaming the pasture keeping her peace. Adam thought on that. He'd have to keep going on and on with his thoughts, for he didn't dare let his heart take over or he'd find himself crying for sure.

Uncle Windy never cried. He was a man of laughter, a great storyteller, loved by everyone. He had never given in to hard times or hardships. Adam supposed it was different for women. Uncle Windy's wife, Aunt Dory, would weep until Uncle Windy cheered her. Aunt Viv, Uncle Burl's wife, was stronger maybe, but she gave in to hard times by becoming as hard as the times themselves. Adam had always hoped to be jovial and happy, just like his Uncle Windy, when he grew up.

At last, he felt ready to leave the warm smell of cow behind him and go into the house to face Aunt Dory and G-Mama. He found Aunt Dory being comforted by her oldest daughter, who stopped her crooning for a second to ask G-Mama, "Who's staying with you tonight, G-Mama? You don't need to be alone tonight?"

G-Mama's answer was sharp and sure. "I've been alone a good share of my life. Aloneness and me are friends."

Aunt Dory said, "But G-Mama, if you refuse to come along home with us, and that I understand because of the far distance, you got to say yes to someone staying. It ain't the same kind of aloneness, oh, Lord no it ain't."

Adam said not a word but simply took G-Mama's hand. He understood.

G-Mama said, "If someone's got to stay, leave Big Adam's little ones. They got enough sense to leave me settle things inside myself without talking every second."

Aunt Viv had overheard and came quickly to agree with G-Mama. "It makes sense, Dory. We all need thinking time. I'll let Eva stay if you let Little Adam. G-Mama, you'll want Burl and Windy brought back to your house, I reckon, since it's halfway between

7

our places and nearby the graveyard. Burl would want to be buried next to his pa and real mama, I know. How you feel about it, Dory? The sheriff needs to know."

Aunt Dory nodded agreement.

So it was that Adam slept in the same house with his twin sister, Eva, for the first time in the seven years since their parents had died. He slept on the cot in the living room, and Eva slept with G-Mama on the old-fashioned high wooden-posted bed. Eva had a nightmare that night and kept screaming about a monster. G-Mama was having a fare-thee-well of a time trying to get her back to sleep.

"Shut up and go to sleep, Eva!" Adam finally yelled as forcefully as he could. He figured she must be used to having Aunt Viv do that, but it didn't help.

"The child's grieving. Leave her be," shouted back G-Mama.

Things were quiet for a couple of minutes and then Eva came sneaking into the living room next to Adam's cot. "Little Adam, I cain't get to sleep. I think G-Mama is grieving. She's crying. I cain't go back to sleep without that monster coming. Can I stay here? Are you grieving, Little Adam?"

"I ain't crying."

Eva whispered, "I ain't crying anymore either. You know something, Little Adam? I never grieved when our mama and daddy died."

"Course you didn't, you were only three. Let's not talk about that."

"What can we talk about? I ain't sleepy at all anymore."

"Well, you better get sleepy!" Adam said it firmly. "And don't look on the dark side. Aunt Dory is still alive and that's something to be thankful for."

"I don't live with Aunt Dory."

"Well, Aunt Viv is alive." No sooner had he said the words than he somehow knew that they were wrong and he added, "You can come visit us a lot. Aunt Dory would like that." That's all he said, but it seemed to make Eva feel better, and she crept back towards G-Mama.

It would be up to him to cheer Aunt Dory now that Uncle Windy was gone. It wouldn't be an easy job since Aunt Dory was prone to sadness, but he would sure give it all he had. Adam was determined to grow up laughing just like Uncle Windy. It was good for a body, especially when it wasn't proper for a man to cry in the first place.

Eva never made it all the way back to G-Mama's before she turned and came crawling back beside Adam's cot again. "Little Adam, I'm going to be left all alone again. I just know it. I feel it already."

"You just feel that way right now. But you still got Aunt Viv. You still got a home. Now, think on that."

He tried to sound cheerful but he himself was sure glad he didn't have to depend on Aunt Viv. He wished he could say something better to Eva, who was really looking like an orphan now, sitting there in the moonlight, thin as tissue paper in her little white underslip. He reached out and touched a strain of straggly dark hair and said, "Look, I promise you, you won't ever be left alone. I'm your brother. You always got me. And I'll get you adopted, and there'll be love and laughter all the time. Okay?"

This time Eva went all the way back to G-Mama's bed. He heard the bedsprings break as she crawled in. And he heard the creaking for another good fifteen or twenty minutes before she finally settled down to go to sleep. So now he could drop off himself. Right now he couldn't worry about how he could keep his promise to Eva. What she needed was a loving caring grown-up around, and somehow he'd have to find that person for her. One thing he could do for her right off was teach her how to go to sleep fast. That was something useful he had perfected for himself.

two

It must have been all the sleep he lost on account of having to take care of Eva that made him wake up so late the next day. He got up to find no one in the house. Finally he looked out the kitchen window and saw G-Mama with her head pressed against the Jersey's flank, milking. Eva was standing next to her, sweeping away flies with a willow branch. He figured there was no call to draw attention to his late sleeping by asking for something to eat, so he grabbed a biscuit off the table and sopped up the gravy that was left in the bowl, drank two dippers of water and called it a meal. As the dipper hit the pail to rest, it made a rattling sound, and that sound was echoed again by someone rattling the front screen door.

"G-Mama!" an old man's voice called. Adam ran to the door.

It was Mr. Kirkwood who ran the general store. "Hey, young feller, G-Mama around?"

"Out milking."

"H-m-m-m. You're about big enough to be out milking for her, I'd say." The old man made little grating sounds across the bottom of the screen with his cane as he talked.

He wore ancient Sunday-pants that drew tight across his knees and bagged loose in back, along with a red flannel shirt. Even in the early part of the day it was too hot to be wearing wool church pants and a flannel shirt. And anytime was too early to be sticking his nose where it didn't belong.

The very idea of coming up and trying to make a person feel unmanly when he was only letting G-Mama milk her own cow. Adam was just about to give him the kind of answer he deserved when Eva popped up right beside him.

"You his sister?" the old man asked Eva and then continued without waiting for an answer. "You're both the same size. You twins? What's your names?"

Adam was surprised. People seldom ever thought of him and Eva as brother and sister because of Eva being of dark hair and brown eyes like their mama and him being fair like their daddy. And the way they lived in different homes, more like cousins, no one ever suspected them of being twins. It pleased Adam that the old man had spotted it so easily.

"I'm Little Adam, the son of Big Adam, G-Mama's

12

youngest boy, and this is my sister, Eva Braggs."
Adam used a much politer tone than he'd originally
intended.

The old man did a little soft shuffle with his feet
and chuckled. "That makes you Adam and Eve, don't
it?"

"My name's Eva," said Eva. "They called me after
my mama, Evangeline."

"You don't say? With twins, they might have
knowed people would hook them names up like that.
Anyway, it's unusual for a girl to be named for her
mama." Then he added in a pitying voice, "You poor
orphans."

Drat it! Adam moved protectively close to Eva and
was just starting to give the old man back some of his
same sass when G-Mama's demanding voice interrupted. "Kirkwood, you say something to upset my
grandchildren?"

The old man fanned out the front of his red flannel
shirt to relieve the sticky hotness, waved his cane in
G-Mama's face and said, "I never said a word. Nary a
word. So calm down."

Adam looked at his tiny G-Mama who was full of
fight and knew he didn't have to worry about her. He
couldn't help wishing that Aunt Dory could be more
like that. It was G-Mama's enemies that needed pro-
tection. Adam felt moved to save the old man's hide
by shouting, "He never said a thing to upset me, G-
Mama, nor Eva either. Did he, Eva?"

Eva just brushed some dirt off Adam's overalls and took her time answering. Finally she said, "He called us poor orphans, but I don't know him, G-Mama, so his words cain't possibly upset me."

"Well, I know him!" G-Mama stated. "And he's the type of man that doesn't know when he's already said enough. He's . . ."

"Now G-Mama, calm down. I come to see if I could bring you anything from my store. You know what I got is yours for the asking. You'll be having a real crowd coming on you tonight. I'm mighty sorry about your boys."

G-Mama stood still as if she were doing some hard thinking. Then she said, "My first thought was to say, 'No thanks,' for we got leftovers setting out in the pump house on the ice they brought in from the back of Windy's truck, but on second thought I say bring me four pounds of cheese. All my boys loved to see cheese appear on the table. Their pa used to bring it sometimes as a treat in spite of tight money. This'll be the last meal I spread in their honor. I'll get you the money. Eva, bring me the cracker tin above the warming closet."

"There ain't no charge. If you want four pounds of cheese, though that be a lot, it's exactly how much I'll fetch back to you." Mr. Kirkwood left at once to carry out his promise. By using his cane to knock aside anything that came into his path, he weaved his way quickly out of the yard.

14

"That was right nice of him to make that offer," Adam said.

G-Mama didn't even check to see if Mr. Kirkwood was out of hearing distance to say, "Not as generous as he makes it sound, though I appreciate the offer. He thinks I'll weaken. He's been after me to marry him for the last twenty years, ever since your granddaddy died. But I wouldn't have him for a husband. He grates on me. Why, that man wouldn't let me breathe without telling me which way to draw my breath. If I've told him no once, I've told him a million times. He's too old for me. He knows that!"

"You seventy-five, G-Mama?" Adam asked knowing that she was.

"Yep!"

"How old's he? Ninety?"

"Nope, but he looks it and acts it. Using a cane, and him only seventy-six. If you ever see me using a cane, tell me my time is up and take me out behind the barn and shoot me."

Adam started to laugh, but he saw that G-Mama's silly words upset Eva. Eva said, "G-Mama, I don't like you talking about being shot. It ain't respectful with my uncles dead."

G-Mama stood strong and straight and bit her lips to keep them from trembling. Tears sparkled in her eyes, and she just stood there openly letting them spill over on her cheeks.

"Eva, G-Mama don't actually mean it like that. She

talks tough because she practically run the sawmill over at Townly. You was the bookkeeper there until it shut down and you married Granddaddy, right?"

G-Mama looked thankful for the help. "He's right, Eva. I do run off at the mouth at times. Maybe it is because I worked with tough men and maybe it isn't. I don't know. I do know I got by, and I refused to marry a one of them men because I was waiting to marry for love. Oh Eva, I know my boys are dead. But dead don't end love. I've loved 'em since they was ornery young men driving their daddy wild. I was fifty-three and your granddaddy forty-one when he set me a bargain. Said he'd forget my age if I was willing to take them boys and him too. I said it was a bargain if he'd shave off his mustache. I got my family all at once, and they're leaving me the same way."

Adam's heart ached for G-Mama. He tried to think of something to comfort her. "Uncle Windy told me that the Lord gave him Big Adam for a brother and the Lord had His right to take Big Adam away too. That help you, G-Mama?"

"It does, Little Adam. I know it's Him who takes. I believe in a loving God. That's an honest fact. I don't mean to be disputed on it." With those last sassy words, G-Mama was back to being her own fighting self again, and Adam felt lighter.

Eva moved her face to one side and kissed the deep brown hand of G-Mama's that lay on her shoulder. "I ain't disputing it."

"I ain't either," said Adam.

So there was no argument then, nor the rest of the day, for G-Mama had said she wished to be near the earth and had put on her bonnet and gone alone into the woods. She took a bucket for gathering herbs and mushrooms. Adam stayed at the house and took charge of greeting the neighbors, who brought gifts of food.

Eva swept every inch of the floor in the cabin's three rooms over and over again. Adam couldn't stop her.

"We got to clean up from one crowd before the next crowd gets here," she said stubbornly.

"That don't make sense, Eva." He certainly would not sweep a floor to have it messed up again right away. So he didn't help Eva. Anyway, that was what Uncle Windy would have called women's work. He sure missed Uncle Windy.

G-Mama got back shortly before dark. Aunt Dory and her family and Aunt Viv and her family had already arrived. Aunt Viv was raging mad when she found G-Mama was out. So the instant G-Mama walked in, she shouted, "With people coming, I'd think you'd stay home."

G-Mama didn't apologize. She just placed the white package she carried in the center of the table and opened it, stood back and admired the four pounds of golden cheese that sat there like a crown. "Met Kirkwood on the way back. This is longhorn. My boys loved longhorn."

Adam reached out to cut a small sliver of cheese

with the butcher knife that he had placed next to a johnnycake. "It's mine and Uncle Windy's favorite, ain't it, Aunt Dory?"

Aunt Dory nodded her head, "Yes, I reckon it was. We never could afford to bring cheese in the house but I reckon when he give you a treat at the store it was this kind."

Adam closed his eyes and again he was standing in a store and reaching into the dime bag of cheese and crackers. He was letting it go into his mouth to rest for long seconds before chewing so he could enjoy the taste and smell longer. Uncle Windy was laughing and saying, "Eat up, boy. I bought it for you to eat."

Eva said, "I never tasted cheese in my whole life!" She began reaching and grabbing for the small piece Adam had cut off.

Aunt Viv swatted Adam's hand as he reached back for a second sliver. "G-Mama, you'd best be facing the facts of life. You shouldn't be squandering your money on cheese when you ain't got no boys left to come sneaking you some cash. You'd do well to return it before Little Adam has it cut up enough so you cain't."

G-Mama said, "I'll worry about the paying for it, Viv. We're going to feed the people who come calling in a fitting way. It's the last time we'll ever set table with my boys in my house."

Aunt Dory started to cry and her oldest daughter

18

came running in from the living room to comfort her. Aunt Viv steeled herself and stood straight and determined in front of G-Mama. "Don't concern yourself, G-Mama. But your time will soon come to miss all the loving care you been getting. Well, me and Dory feel it right now. Windy never let Dory know his business affairs and right this minute she don't know if there is money to pay their grocery bill. Burl was my husband but he had his faults. He and his brothers was a crazy reckless chance-taking lot. What did it get them but dead?"

Adam had seen Aunt Viv mad before. In fact, most every time they had a reunion, she'd get mad before they left for home. Usually because Uncle Burl drank something besides ice water. Right now, this sort of anger was too scary.

"I'm not hungry," announced Adam. He grabbed Eva's arm and scuttled out of the house. Angry words continued inside the house just beyond hearing. Adam looked at Eva, expecting to see a scared face, but he saw a curious one. She was pointing at a black truck coming down the road.

"The sheriff is coming again. I better warn G-Mama so's she'll stop fighting." Eva ran inside.

"Howdy, Sheriff," Adam said politely. "You want to see G-Mama again?"

"Howdy, folks," said Erica Wheeler.

Adam turned to see three of his cousins coming from beside the house to join him. From inside the

19

house came G-Mama's voice loud enough for people clear on the other side of the woods to hear. "They was my own!"

Erica Wheeler looked to the cousins and said, "Maybe some of you older ones could take the younger ones for a walk for a while. The hearse will be coming along directly. I got to go inside and talk to G-Mama, and it looks like I was right to come out a bit early." She spoke expecting to be obeyed, which is the habit of a law person, Adam reckoned. She marched right in through the front door, and Adam ran, against his cousins' protests, right in behind her. After all, Eva was in there in the middle of the fracas.

No one seemed to pay any attention to the fact that the sheriff had come in. Eva was holding G-Mama's hand and G-Mama was saying, "God gave me the boys. I got every right to be called their God-Mama, and what God seals, is."

Adam wanted to give sanction to what G-Mama said and he very much wanted her to notice that Erica Wheeler was there listening. He shouted, "That's right. Uncle Windy says it may not stand up in a court of law, but loving and caring is binding in itself."

Heads turned and Aunt Viv jerked Eva to one side and then directed an order at Adam. "Hold your tongue, child, and leave grown-up talk to grown-ups. Howdy, Sheriff."

Aunt Dory said, "Ain't a one of us going to argue your point one mite, Little Adam. G-Mama knows that. No one means to argue that they were her boys."

It seemed to quieten G-Mama to have Dory talk soft like that. "Thank you. I know both of you lost a husband. And we're all troubled in mind over how the accident could have happened. Howdy, Ericky."

"Howdy," said the sheriff and reached out to shake G-Mama's hand. "G-Mama, I guess your boys were happy to the end, and that's more than some."

Windy's second oldest daughter said, "Likely they was spinning yarns, and Uncle Burl started laying bets that he could beat the train across the tracks." She caught her breath short as all the women gasped. Adam knew they were scared of her being so honest right in front of the sheriff. He felt sorry for her predicament.

So as to help her out, he said, "It was probably true. I been in the truck when they've beat a train. I never was scared, for Uncle Burl was a good driver. He could stop on a dime, if he needed to." It didn't seem to help any to say what he said, for both G-Mama and Aunt Dory moaned.

Sheriff Erica Wheeler said, "We could guess forever but there is no point to it. We'd still have a bunch of probabilities. Fact is, we've got little fact to go on. G-Mama, you know that Burl had just bought two quarts of apricot brandy to take back to the re-

21

union. No law, neither yours nor mine, could have stopped him. People live and die being whatever they are. I've come to pay my respects and to let you know that the hearse . . ."

Aunt Viv interrupted. "We're glad you come. We got business we need to discuss. If we do it in front of the law, G-Mama will have to listen. There won't be no compensation money coming from the railroad if Burl was carrying liquor. And money is the issue we must all face. It's always been the issue, I reckon. Burl never was practical and neither was Windy, for that matter."

Adam shouted, "Don't you talk about my Uncle Windy. He was, too, practical!"

"Shut up, Little Adam, when adults are speaking! Now as I was saying, Sheriff, we got to manage somehow. It won't be easy. I went to the telephone office last night and placed a long-distance call to my oldest boy in California." Aunt Viv looked sideways at G-Mama. "Be it the boys could get G-Mama a phone, we are still without one, so I had to ask the operator to send someone to fetch my boy and have him call back. He did and there on the spot offered to send me and my kids bus fare to San Francisco. It's decent of him, but I couldn't ask him to take on us and Big Adam's kid, especially when Eva's got Aggie, her own mother's sister, wanting her."

It was Eva who gasped this time. Adam found it difficult not to do so himself.

22

Viv went right on talking. "While I was already there at the phone company, I placed a call to the store where Aggie worked, the last I heard. I told them to have Aggie call me back, and I'd wait for the call. Well, she did, and she not only said she'd take Eva but would take Little Adam too, like she'd wanted to do when Evangeline and Big Adam was killed."

Adam did gasp. "Aunt Dory, you don't . . . I got to stay with you. You need me to take care of you. I'm old enough right now!"

Aunt Dory's soft words drowned out the horrible words from Aunt Viv. "Little Adam is staying with me. We'll manage."

Aunt Dory's oldest daughter left her job of setting the table and ran to her mother. She pushed Adam aside as she pleaded, "How, Mama, how? Aunt Viv is right. You owe Daddy's note to the bank. My Weldon cain't pay it. It's hard times, Mama. Let Little Adam go to his Aunt Aggie. He'll be in good hands, and I know I can get you a job cleaning at the air base. Come on back to Texas with me, Mama. I'm glad I come home for the reunion; now I can take you back as Daddy would have wanted me to do."

G-Mama snapped, "You don't really know this woman Aggie! My boys always managed to hang on; now you women can get a little spunk in your pants and try. No sense to giving up and running scared, sending a child away to a stranger. Never mind! I'll take Eva to raise myself. And, Dory, you can stay home and manage, and you can bring Adam over to visit. Let him know he's a twin. Twins ought to be together. That was one thing my boys did I never approved of—raising these two kids apart. I never could go against the wishes of my boys, but their wives is something else. It's a crime to send Eva off to a stranger. Look, I'll make it legal. I got a few dollars' cash hid out and I can pay for drawing up the adoption papers. Draw 'em up for me, Ericky!"

"G-Mama, we're tired of dreaming and storytelling and laughing," Aunt Viv said angrily. "You're too old and you know it. The law won't allow someone your age to adopt—we found that out seven years ago. We all got to manage the best we can and on scarce little, too. I'm sending Eva to Saint Louis on the train day after tomorrow. If I'm hard, I got your son to thank for the hardness in me. Facing facts never was part of the Braggs family. But the facts are that you're old, seventy-five; Dory's in debt; and Aggie is willing to take them both.

"Age's got nothing to do with it!" said G-Mama. "I could have took care of the kids seven years ago and I can right now. I had the means and the pep then, and I still got both and that's all that counts."

But Adam's heart sank. He knew the law was the law, and if it said G-Mama was too old, there was no getting around it. He'd have to make the best of Aunt Aggie.

24

Aunt Dory put her fingers to her lips and whispered, "Sh-h-h-h, Viv. The kids are hearing too much. I couldn't let Little Adam go off to a stranger."

"A *blood* relative ain't exactly a stranger," said Aunt Viv. "The boy is old enough to share a little of the pain of hard times, same as the rest of us. It's no time to afford generosity. The Braggs boys were generous to a fault. Right now I accept myself as a penniless widow, and I got no money to raise Eva or any other child. You cain't get blood from a turnip!"

Aunt Viv's voice stopped and Adam could hear soft sobs. He looked to find Eva sitting with eyes closed tight trying to hold back tears. He touched her. She whispered, "I told you, Little Adam. I told you I was going to be left alone again. You say loving and caring is binding, but there ain't no loving and caring."

Eva was right. But Aunt Viv was right too, about the money. The men who handled the money were dead. Adam was willing to be a man right now, if need be, but he didn't know how to get money for Aunt Dory. Maybe it'd be more manly to go off to Saint Louis with Eva and let Aunt Dory be free to get the money herself. Eva was going to need someone to be with her. "Aunt Dory, I'm going with Eva until you get money enough to pay up the note to the bank and then some. We'll both come back."

"Little Adam, I won't let you go off to a stranger!"

"Aunt Dory, I can if Eva can. I'll come back when . . ."

It was G-Mama who protested now, "I never deal with ifs or whens. That's not clear thinking."

Erica Wheeler seemed like a mountain of authority as she looked at G-Mama and said, "Sounds to me like the boy is thinking clear enough. He recognizes the facts and he cares for his sister. That's pretty clear thinking under the circumstances."

Adam liked her words but the truth was, he wasn't thinking clearly at all. His thoughts were buzzing around in a mass of confusion. Neither he nor Eva knew what this Aunt Aggie was like. Why, he couldn't really remember his own mother, let alone her sister. The whole thing scared him but he'd best not let Eva know that.

No one spoke for a while until whispers from the front porch told them that the hearse had arrived. Adam looked to the sheriff and said, "I guess me and Eva will take that walk now. I got other things I need to do some clear thinking on." He stood with his sweaty hands on the cool glass doorknob and waited for the nod of approval.

As soon as they were in the safety of the woods, Adam said, "Eva, what I told you the other night is the truth. Every last word of it. I promise you, I'll get you adopted proper so's you won't ever be left alone again like Aunt Viv's doing to you now. I won't let the sun go down in Saint Louis until I see to it that Aunt Aggie adopts you and makes you a true daughter. And there'll be no legal loophole for her to worm through and upset you. There, don't you feel better?"

"I don't know, Little Adam. You cain't *make* grown-ups do nothing."

"I can. You don't know grown-ups' ways. You wait and see. As a matter of fact, Eva Braggs, you don't know my ways very well either."

three

Adam kissed Uncle Windy good-bye at the funeral
and kissed Aunt Dory good-bye at the house. Aunt
Dory refused to go along to the train stop, saying she
never wanted to be near another train in all her life.
Adam had been friends with trains all of his life and it
was hard to stop liking them now because of a terrible accident, but he respected how Aunt Dory felt.

Aunt Dory's married girl took him and Eva to the
train stop. G-Mama went too, but she refused to kiss
or be kissed. She merely said, "Stand your ground,
Little Adam. You too, Eva. If that Aunt Aggie of
yours is no good, look up the sheriff in Saint Louis
and tell him I'm waiting."

Adam took courage from her words but they
seemed to upset Eva. Eva was having problems
knowing G-Mama's ways.

"Nothing's going to go wrong, Eva. Aunt Aggie is blood kin and she'll treat us nice. Anyway, even if she didn't it is only for a short while. Aunt Dory'll have her head above water pretty soon on that bank note, and she'll send for me, and you can come back with me. We can put up with anything for a while. So it don't matter how things are, one way or another. Say good-bye to G-Mama, okay?"

Black engine number 99 came charging to a stop, its bell clanging and steam puffing until it gave a great sigh and stood still. Suddenly there they were, the two of them on a green velvet seat trying to see G-Mama through thick green curtains that refused to part. Strangers all in front of them and behind them. It was spooky as a nightmare sitting there not knowing anyone.

He scooted closer to Eva and said, "Trains are fun. Ain't it something? We don't know nobody, and it ain't bad at all."

Eva was still watching to see where the conductor placed their cardboard box of belongings. She said, "It's scary in this dark train."

"Oh, it ain't. It ain't scary a bit. Want me to tell you a story?"

"No, Little Adam, I want to tell you something. This is a real story, and for some reason, I'm remembering it awfully good right now. Once, long ago, when Uncle Burl took me to live with him and Aunt Viv, Aunt Viv ripped my wet pants off me and

29

screamed. 'Wet your pants and you a three-year-old? I'll put a diaper on you if you're going to act like a baby.' That was seven years ago and I can still remember it. It was scary then too. I hated that diaper and I hated my mama and daddy for going away and never coming back. I hated them for leaving me with Aunt Viv. I didn't know they were dead. I guess I didn't know what dead was."

Adam sat silent for a moment. A woman with very wavy hair looked back over her seat at them. He wondered if she had heard Eva. It would surely leave that woman guessing if she did hear, for never had anyone told a story like that to Adam before.

He whispered so that woman in front of them could not hear. "Eva, I hate that story. Stories are supposed to be funny and make you laugh."

Gosh darn it, why couldn't she remember nice things like he did about Uncle Windy and laughter? Maybe it was the pounding away of the big train wheels on the track, but his own mind started remembering some bad things too.

Uncle Windy and Aunt Dory were laughing at him, and Uncle Windy called him piss-pants; swatted his bottom. In his memory, not only was Uncle Windy laughing but he heard other laughter too. It came from a tall blond man who at another time had swatted his bottom and said, "You don't need to come along for soda pop. It's too cold for soda pop in the middle of winter."

Then the tall man grabbed a pretty lady around the waist. She was dressed in a green Christmas dress and had a red scarf. He could still see the furry boots she wore to keep out the cold. The man said, "I want some time alone with my Evangeline." And he took Mama away to the car, singing all the while, "Evangeline, Evangeline, I'll make you mine, Evangeline."

Adam, too, had hated that tall Daddy who never brought Mama back. And he hated Eva for making him remember.

"Eva, it ain't right to hate the dead, for goodness' sakes. I love Uncle Windy, and he's dead. G-Mama loves Granddaddy, and he's been dead a long time. Now get your mind off it and let's talk about something else."

But just giving an order did not make Eva stop. For the rest of the trip, she yapped her head off about what Aunt Aggie was probably like, and about the times Aunt Viv had beaten her, and about how she imagined the funeral must have been for Big Adam and Mama. At least he had gotten her to keep her voice low by staying cuddled close and answering her only in whispers. The wavy-haired woman turned again to look at them like that and said, "How cute." Then she never turned around again.

Eva continued to whisper how she was sure that Mama's casket had been white and not gray like the uncles' and that Mama's dress was white and . . .

31

well, he just turned off his listening after that. He pretended to listen, though, else Eva would have been even more scared than she already was. Let her talk on.

Eva ate one of the cheese sandwiches that G-Mama had put in a sack for them, but Adam couldn't eat. He was trying too hard to hear while the conductor called out places at each train stop. He sure didn't want to miss Saint Louis. How could Eva be hungry at a time like this? And her eating didn't slow down her talking very much.

Occasionally Eva's chatter would stop and she'd ask, "Don't you ever feel like that, Little Adam?" or, "You remember that, Little Adam?" and he'd answer, "I'm your twin, ain't I?"

Once he answered in this manner and found that he'd agreed that being a twin meant he also needed to use the toilet. He asked the conductor for Eva. They had a toilet right there on a moving train.

Finally, the conductor called out "Saint Louis," and they got off the train along with everyone else. Eva stopped her talking. At first he was glad, for it was noisy in the train yard and he couldn't have heard her very well, and besides there was a stream-lined silver zephyr on a track across the way and it was something to see.

So was the inside of the train station something to see with its mile-high ceilings and stone carvings all over the place. He ought to stop gawking and start trying to spot Aunt Aggie. As he and Eva proceeded farther into the station carrying their box of belongings, the twine bit into his palm and he said, "I think you need to rest a minute, Eva."

She seemed glad enough to set the box down but she didn't say a word. He wished she would take up her talking again instead of standing there looking dumb and scared.

"Hey, this is a pretty fair-sized building, ain't it?" he asked.

"Where is Aunt Aggie?" Eva whispered. "Aunt Viv said she looked like Mama, but I don't know what Mama looked like."

"Back there on the train you didn't have any trouble remembering all sorts of things when you were only three. Now try to remember. I know she had black hair like you.

"I cain't remember nothing, Little Adam. Here comes a woman with two kids. You suppose she has kids?"

"She could have. They could be almost grown. Remember Big Adam and Mama married late. That ain't her. She's going on past us. Maybe she don't know us either. Hey, EVA BRAGGS, hold this for me will you, EVA BRAGGS?" Adam practically shouted out Eva's name.

"I don't mind holding your sack awhile, ADAM BRAGGS. My arms ain't tired at all, ADAM BRAGGS!"

33

Adam couldn't believe it. Eva was just about reading his mind. He wondered if it was because they were twins. Seemed like he might have heard that twins thought alike; could tell what the other was thinking even if they were a thousand miles apart.

The dark-haired woman and her two kids stopped a minute to stare but walked right on. But coming up fast were two policemen. Maybe it was against the law to shout in this big fancy Saint Louis station.

"Adam and Eva Braggs? We've been looking for you. Lucky you were talking so loud. Your aunt never gave us much of a description. Said you were twins. You sure don't look it."

Adam didn't know what to say. Something was very wrong here. Why would the law be here to meet them instead of Aunt Aggie? The last time a law officer appeared suddenly, it was Sheriff Erica Wheeler with bad news.

Eva pulled the sleeve of the policeman who had spoken and said, "Our Aunt Aggie ain't coming for us, is she?"

"Eva's got a big imagination. She thinks of all kinds of stuff to worry about. She . . ."

The policeman sort of bent down and cradled Eva against him and said softly, "That's right, honey. But you're going to be taken care of. We got a nice big house with a lot of other little girls you can be with."

"Where's Aunt Aggie? Why didn't she come like she said?" Adam demanded.

The policeman that was holding on to Eva just went kind of pale and left it to the other one to answer.

"Your aunt is in a pretty sorry fix herself," he said. "She called us to come for you because she can't take care of you like she wanted."

"If you'll tell us where she lives then I reckon we can take ourselves out to her house," Adam said.

"It's not that she can't come." The policeman seemed hard put to explain. "It's that she is not coming."

Eva screeched, "We're orphans a third time, Little Adam. Oh, Little Adam, you ought not to have made that promise to me. You cain't make grown-ups do what you wish." She started to cry softly.

Adam felt strong and determined. "Let *me* talk to Aunt Aggie!" he demanded of the policeman.

"Look, lad, your Aunt Aggie is a widow and has five kids of her own and is about to marry a workingman with six. He put his foot down about you two adding to the number when she told him about her intentions and her promise to take you. Now you understand that, lad? You're old enough to know we're in the middle of hard times. We're doing all we can for you. We tried talking to your aunt, but she wouldn't even give us an address. She said that she'd weaken if she saw you and then she hung up before I could say anything else. She was sorry, lad. She said so."

"No, no, she ain't sorry," said Adam. "No one who is really sorry goes ahead and does a thing."

The policeman didn't argue. He just guided them along to a police car. As the car drove through the big city, Eva finished off the cheese sandwiches that were in their sack.

Finally the policeman brought the car to a stop in front of a big house. A big dark three-story house with pointed roofs jutting above the concrete fence that surrounded it. It looked awful. And Adam knew what it was.

What kind of protector of Eva was he? He had opened his big mouth and yelled their names in that train station and had gotten the two of them hauled in by the law. He, who had promised Eva he'd have her adopted proper by sundown, had managed to get them both carted off to an orphan asylum!

four

"Sir, I think I better call G-Mama. Aunt Dory don't have a phone but G-Mama does because she lives back in the woods, and my uncles put it in to check on her."

"Now lad, whatever are you talking about?" the policeman asked as he was lifting Eva out of the police car.

Eva said, "Little Adam always stretches a story."

"Eva," Adam scolded and then to the policeman explained, "I'm telling you that G-Mama said if anything went wrong we was to locate the sheriff of Saint Louis and tell him that she was waiting. You're about like a sheriff. You could let me call G-Mama, for I know that she's waiting."

"Is the boy talking about your grandmother?" the policeman asked Eva.

Eva answered, "No. Our real grandma died before either of us was born."

Adam knew that he shouldn't have let Eva answer. He said, "We both was born at the same time. What Eva means is that G-Mama was there already when we got born. The way G-Mama tells it is that what the good Lord binds . . ."

The yard lights switched on at the big house and a voice cut in. "I told you there's no more room. There simply is no more room!" A fat jelly-skinned woman came through the gate and Adam's explanation went unheard.

One of the policemen said, "This is Eva. That one, Adam. And any kind of temporary space is room. Just stick them together. They're twins. Our orders are to leave them here."

"I don't argue with the law." The woman threw out her hands. "I guess I'll find some space on the floor. Last night we got fourteen from one family. They were brought to us in blankets. Their house burned, and the mother had a heart attack. Five of the children was the woman's sisters' kids that she'd taken in. We only had bed space for eight and put the rest on pallets. I guess two more pallets won't make any difference. Go on up the steps; I'll follow."

Adam was tired. Tireder than he'd ever been in his whole life. He guessed Eva was used to obeying orders from Aunt Viv, for she quickly started on ahead. Adam followed her, but the policeman stopped him for a minute.

38

"Look, lad, your Aunt Aggie did *call*. She didn't leave you stranded. You try to get along here. Your Aunt Aggie gave us the name of the woman who called her, and we managed to place a call through to the central at the Fisk Phone Company. It seems that Mrs. Vivian Braggs is leaving town, and your other kin too. Now don't go making out to these folks here that you got a grandma waiting. Mrs. Braggs says your grandma has been dead quite sometime."

Adam had been accused of stretching the truth before, and now this policeman thought him a liar and just turned and walked away, not waiting for an explanation. Left him standing there in the foyer of an orphan asylum with a jelly-skinned woman. Adam was too stunned to open his mouth.

"I'm Miss Lucille, your housemother," said the woman.

"Not *our* housemother. We ain't staying!" Adam's voice came back in a rush and he ran to the door to stop the policeman. He just had to explain. The door was locked. He turned around and stared at Miss Lucille and Eva. A tiny whimper came from a closet next to him. Quickly Miss Lucille jerked open the closet door. "So, there you are! We've looked all over for you!"

A very small boy about four years old with nothing on but some light blue pants sat huddled there. He whimpered louder now at being found. Miss Lucille took his hand and pulled him out. He kicked and screamed at her, "Take me to Mommy. Take me to

Mommy," so loud that soon the foyer was packed with what seemed like hundreds of boys and girls of all sizes. They were yelling questions, letting their excitement get higher and higher, shouting "Who found him?" "Where was he?" "You've found Honcie!"

Miss Lucille was shouting back at them. "Get to your chores. Move now. Come on." No one moved. It was starting to feel awfully tight in that front foyer, and almost impossible for him to keep hold on Eva's hand. Then things started loosening up; he wondered why until he felt a sudden sting on his backside. Miss Lucille had a ruler in her hand and was swatting away with it at anyone within range.

Adam pulled Eva into the corner by the door and shouted to the bunch of children going back inside. "We're not staying here. We're leaving right now."

One big boy stopped and grabbed the other end of the ruler that Miss Lucille held and, ignoring her efforts to pull loose, announced, "You're staying. You're too old for anyone to want to adopt." He let go of the ruler and let Miss Lucille swing at him again and went on in with the rest.

Miss Lucille said, "I tell them time and again that we all got to get along or things are a mess. Now this is the Weston Home named after Senator Weston, who used to own this estate before he gave it to the state for an orphanage. You'll like it here, but the first thing you must know is that everybody's got to work together."

She stuck her ruler back into a long narrow apron pocket, very much like the pencil pocket on Adam's bib overalls. Eva was attempting to open the locked front door. Adam gave it a couple of hard pulls too. Sometimes it seems a door is locked when it's only stuck. It was locked. Well, it better come unlocked, for no woman with a soft roll of fat above the waist could hold him inside an orphan asylum, even if she did have a ruler dangling in her apron pocket.

Surprisingly Miss Lucille came, took out her key, and then helped them pull the big door open. "It's still light enough out to see the grounds. We got four vegetable gardens. We stretch the state's dollar a little farther that way. When everybody helps it keeps hands busy and tempers intact."

One garden was a turnip patch, another a potato patch. The other two had mixed vegetables and looked like they could stand a good cultivating. Adam said as much.

Miss Lucille agreed and said, "You sure can give us a hand with that tomorrow."

He hated to cut short her friendliness, but she had to understand how things were. "I'd help if I was staying, but I ain't. You got a telephone here?"

The answer to that question was a tremendous sound of an electric bell. "Time for baths and teeth-brushing," announced Miss Lucille, and she started pulling them back towards the door.

"I don't have no toothbrush," said Eva.

"Did you forget it?"

Adam answered for his sister. "No, we didn't forget it. We don't own such. We don't need one."

"But your teeth are so white."

"Course they are. We don't dip snuff, chew tobacco, and we're not old."

Miss Lucille stopped at the door. "But surely you take baths. And you must take your turn. Since you were not here to sign up, you'll be last tonight. Eva, you'll be last tomorrow night. Tonight is boys' night; tomorrow, girls'. After that you can sign up for turns."

"No need. We ain't staying. I'll just come in long enough to use your phone."

Miss Lucille answered as she took out her key to open the big door again. "The phone belongs to our headmaster, Mr. Clearset, and no one goes there to use it without permission. It's after hours now. He lives in the senator's carriage house out back. I'll take you to see him tomorrow. Now let's make you some pallets. If I can find two more blankets," she said as she rummaged in the top of the foyer closet.

Eva started peeping into the front room. She turned back and whispered, "Little Adam, it's like a family reunion. Look!"

"It ain't a family reunion, Eva. At a family reunion you got family; these are all strangers." He shouldn't have pointed that out to Eva, but suddenly the strangeness of it all had totally reared up and stolen away his spunk. He felt tired again.

Too tired to argue. He let Miss Lucille give him a blanket and order him to bed down in a long front room that held twelve cots, four pallets and a large fancy fireplace. The walls were dirty white and bare. Not a calendar or a church picture on them. Adam didn't fight or yell when this woman told Eva she couldn't sleep near him but had to go upstairs with the other girls. He felt blank and wordless. But he never cried, just took his bath and obeyed. Plenty of others were crying and whimpering until the noise was interrupted by someone yelling, "Honcie is gone again! Let's all look for Honcie!"

The old floorboards on the stairs creaked as they all spread out to search. Sometime later, maybe around midnight, they found Honcie hiding behind a trunk under his sister's bed upstairs. Eva was up there on a pallet near that same bed.

She whispered to Adam. "I knew where he was. But he needs to sleep here; he has nightmares too. My nightmare's already come back, filling this place with its monster ugliness. Little Adam, will you just talk, so I'll know you're downstairs?"

"I don't expect they'll allow loud talking but I'll whistle softly. Just listen and you'll know, okay? You feel better, Eva?"

She did.

Adam whistled until sometime later when he must have fallen asleep.

When he woke up he was well aware of the fact that he hadn't had a thing to eat since he left G-

Mama's. He guessed they'd gotten to the orphanage too late for food last night. He might as well eat a good-sized breakfast before he demanded to use the phone to call G-Mama.

Everybody got a tin plate with dividers and a fork and a spoon. They didn't need the fork. A man so fat you couldn't tell if he was wearing a belt was scooping up big globs of mush from a huge iron kettle and socking it onto their plates. Everybody had to put on their own milk and sugar.

The milk was blinky, which tempted Adam to take some sugar, but he never had been one to eat a whole lot of sugar on things. He'd trade candy anytime for a good piece of cheese. He was like his Uncle Windy when it came to that.

The thought of Uncle Windy and Aunt Dory made him get choked on his mush and splutter loudly. He began talking loudly so they would all think it was his natural voice and not sobs they heard.

"You better shut up," whispered the boy next to him; it was the same big guy that had grabbed Miss Lucille's ruler. "Mr. Clearset don't let us talk or make noise during meals."

The big boy was right. It was pretty quiet. For so many children, it was awfully quiet. "Where's Mr. Clearset?" Adam whispered.

The big boy nodded towards the great fat man. That big man had big muscles too. Adam did reckon it might be rough just to go up to him and demand the use of his phone for an expensive long-distance phone call.

"Mr. Clearset's a mean one, huh?" he asked.

The big boy's answer came back as hot as the touch of a lamp chimney. "There are thirty-two kids to make mind. Who wouldn't be mean?"

Adam said no more but watched as Mr. Clearset threw the last glob of mush on Honcie's plate. Then Mr. Clearset put down the long-handled serving spoon and walked from table to table, giving out work assignments. Miss Lucille followed him, making notes. "Sweeping. Darning socks." He gave orders to the girls first. He stopped by Eva. "You write?"

Eva nodded.

"Got a neat hand?"

Eva nodded.

"Go with Miss Lucille and the girls to address envelopes."

"Cleaning boots. Polishing shoes." He gave orders to the boys. Adam waited for him to get close to his table so he could quickly tell him that he wasn't staying and needed to use his phone.

"Shovel coal!" boomed Mr. Clearset.

"I'm supposed to cultivate the garden," Adam found himself saying instead of asking to use the phone.

"You're supposed to do whatever the state says you're to do. And as far as you're concerned, sonny, I'm the state! You the new one?"

Adam nodded.

Miss Lucille said, "I told the policeman we were crowded and had no more beds."

Mr. Clearset gave his attention to Miss Lucille. "Nor funds," he said. "Those smart-aleck cops don't try. Maybe they'd like to rake up the fifty grand it'd take to get this place up to standards. They say anything about helping process them? I got paper work up to my eyeballs as it is and they keep bringing them in. There's a limit!"

Adam felt buoyed up now, for Mr. Clearset ought to be mighty happy to know he and Eva were leaving. "Look, mister, all we need is . . ."

"No talking in the dining hall!" boomed Mr. Clearset. And he moved on muttering, "Smart-aleck kid, got to learn to obey rules. I run a good home in spite of all."

To help run that home, Adam and five other boys shoveled coal from the pile on the driveway into the chute that led to the coal bin. It took all morning. He kept hoping Miss Lucille would come check out their work so he could make her keep her promise about taking him to see Mr. Clearset; then he'd use the phone. She never showed up. He had an idea to hop right over that concrete fence and catch a freight train to southeast Missouri, but Eva would be left somewhere inside that big house addressing envelopes.

It made him mad. Good and mad. He whammed

46

the shovel hard into the coal pile and said, "Why don't they use wood for cooking like common folks? It's a lot cleaner!"

One of the new boys readily agreed with him, but Adam chose not to talk any further. He bore the rest of the morning with slow draining patience.

For the noon meal they had bread and butter and cocoa. All they wanted as long as it lasted. But nothing else. He wondered when they ever ate the vegetables, but since he wasn't allowed to talk, he never asked. He didn't have to wonder long.

After lunch, Mr. Clearset pronounced his work assignment. "Peeling turnips. Miss Lucille will keep check on you. I want you to all work together, and we'll get along just fine." Mr. Clearset left then and let the talking begin.

Most of the talk was complaining about how hard it was to peel with a dull case knife. Adam didn't complain, for he figured that he now had a fair chance of talking to Miss Lucille and also he was going to get to talk to Eva. The girls had been assigned to peel potatoes nearby.

Eva spotted him and came over to whisper, "I'm starving, Little Adam. And I'm scared to sleep here another night. We're prisoners here."

"Worse than prisoners. Drat it, I need to get to that phone!" He said it pretty loud and that scared Eva more, and she started to cry.

"Dad blast it, Eva. I've told you not to cry."

47

"What do you want me to laugh at, Little Adam?"

He couldn't answer that. He didn't want to answer that. Even Uncle Windy would be hard put to answer that one. It made him good and mad again. He dug into another turnip so fiercely that even with a dull case knife he cut his finger. Blood got all over the turnip. Then he began to laugh. "Hey, look, Eva, you can too get blood from a turnip. Aunt Viv said it cain't be done, but look."

Eva laughed. And that made Adam feel so good he shouted the news for everyone to hear. The others caught on to the laughter. Uncle Windy was right. It was the only way to blot out bad times. Adam danced about with the bloody turnip on the point of his knife. Soon everyone in the room was dancing, and having regular fits and spasms of laughing. They all carried a turnip or a potato on the ends of their knives and waved them high in the air.

Even the big boy yelled out, "Anyone know if you can taste a bloody turnip if you have a bad cold?"

Miss Lucille came flying in. Instantly she was swinging her ruler and yelling for "Quiet!"

Adam dropped the bloody turnip into the pot and then she really yelled. "Young man, I must get Mr. Clearset!"

"Blood won't kill nobody." Adam felt cocky and full of vinegar, so to prove his point he began to suck the blood off his finger. She didn't see him. She was running out the back door towards the carriage house.

When Mr. Clearset came in, Adam knew that there would be no use of the phone granted to him. "This the new one again? All right, boy, you'll get no turnips for supper!"

Before Adam could collect his thoughts, Eva stepped out and said, "We don't need your turnips. Our G-Mama has lots of turnips, and she's waiting for us to come home and eat them." What a time Eva had picked to try to help him.

At first Mr. Clearset seemed ready to burst. Then he stopped his anger right in the middle of its swell and asked ever so quietly, "You mean there's someone that wants to claim you? You got a grandmama?"

Quickly, before Eva botched things up again by telling the truth, Adam said, "Sure we have, and she cooks us turnips all the time. Keeps a hill of them all winter long, even makes soup from the sprouts in the spring. She sure does want to claim us!"

Mr. Clearset looked at Miss Lucille. "This a fact?"

"I don't know. The police said their grandparents were dead."

"Them police was mistaken. G-Mama is the alivest thing alive. You can call her. Better yet, you can call the sheriff of Bernie and ask her. You know a sheriff wouldn't lie."

Mr. Clearset looked at Adam long and hard, then took Eva by the hand and left the room. He would be making the phone call and also pumping Eva for information. Adam knew it. He just stood there doing

49

some hard wishing so it might get through to Eva. Come on, Eva, answer right. Now's the time to act like a twin.

The room was silent with everyone, even Miss Lucille, standing waiting. It was taking an awfully long time. Mr. Clearset must be telling Sheriff Erica Wheeler the whole story. But at last he returned, still leading Eva.

Mr. Clearset bellowed, "Sheriff says, 'Send 'em down.' Sheriff'll meet their train. Can't trust the police here anymore. Palming brats off on me when they've got living kin that's willing to take them. Us with no beds. Get their belongings, Lucille."

Eva was smiling as she tagged along after Miss Lucille, who got their box and handed it to her. But she said nothing, so Adam spoke up. "Them's our belongings, all right. Ain't got a thing worth a cent but I wouldn't take a million dollars for them."

Mr. Clearset ignored his words. "I'll drive them to the train. Rest of you get on with your peeling."

The room was silent again as all knives raised. Eva ran ahead of Mr. Clearset and Adam followed. One boy jabbed Adam with his case knife. It hurt. Honcie cried out, "Take me to Mommy. Take me to Mommy!"

Soon as they were safely on the train, Adam said, "Eva, this means that the sheriff will let us stay with G-Mama but it don't mean that G-Mama can adopt you. She's too old. But kinfolk don't need to adopt anyway, right?"

"Wrong. Aunt Viv was my aunt but no blood kin. If you ain't blood kin, you're likely to be let go any-time. G-Mama ain't really no blood kin neither."

"Okay, I'll find a loophole on the age somehow. Okay, Eva?"

five

Erica Wheeler hoisted her gunbelt back up even with her waistline and said, "Well, my duty ain't done until I get you deposited with G-Mama. Hop in the truck, rascals."

Adam and Eva crawled up on the big dusty truck seat and waited while the sheriff got in, pumped the gas pedal a few times and then spun gravel as they headed out of town. It seemed a long time before she was out to the dirt road that led to G-Mama's.

Adam remembered a time when Uncle Windy had a flat tire near the general store and borrowed Mr. Kirkwood's jack and bought soda pop. Made Adam thirsty just to think about the soda pop.

Eva screamed, "See that store, Little Adam? Uncle Burl stopped there once and bought me some orange soda pop."

Now how about that? That was the very color of soda pop his had been. There certainly was something to this business of being twins.

"Did Uncle Burl have a flat tire?" Adam asked.

"Nope. He'd never buy soda pop if he had a flat tire. He'd yell and scream and cause everyone to be scared. He bought soda pop because we were going to G-Mama's house, like we are right now."

Erica Wheeler stepped on the brakes, spun the truck around on the narrow dirt road, barely clearing a road ditch on both sides, and screeched back to a stop in front of the general store. "If getting orange soda pop is part of this trip, I guess I better find a couple of nickels and do my duty right. Hey, Kirkwood, you in there?"

The old man hobbled to the door. "Well, howdy, Sheriff. What brings you out this way? Ain't none of us around here acquainted with money enough to want to rob a bank, ain't got a horse worth stealing, and don't appreciate meddling into family affairs."

"You got three orange soda pops?"

"Sure have. Those G-Mama Braggs' grandchildren?"

Adam didn't bother to answer him. The taste of the pop deserved his whole attention at the moment. Eva had her mouth around the opening of the bottle and the soda pop was going down fast with large gurgling sounds. "Drink it in sips, like this, Eva. It'll make the taste last longer." Eva obeyed without comment and they finished about the same time, which is what twins should do.

When they got to G-Mama's, Erica Wheeler blasted and tooted the horn several times, but no one came to the door. "Well, rascals, here we are. But where is that G-Mama? She knows better than to be hiking about the country when I told her on the phone that I was hauling you kids out here today. Well, get out. We'll round her up."

It took no time at all to get out of the truck and in through the door of the little lean-to attached to the kitchen. G-Mama never let anyone use her front door, for she had it stuffed all around with rags to keep out the cold in the winter and the dust in the summer.

"G-Mama! It's me, Little Adam," he called, but got no answer.

"I'll go get her in a hurry," Eva said, as she ran on into the house.

But Eva never found her, nor did Adam, though they searched all the chicken coops, cow stall, pig pens and even the toilet. Finally Adam came puffing back to join Erica Wheeler and had to admit, "G-Mama ain't here. I hope she's okay."

Erica Wheeler let out a full round of laughter. "G-Mama's okay. She's independent, that's all. It's not the first time I've come calling, and her not be here as expected. She's always got her reasons, and they sound good even to me, once she gets through

54

telling 'em. She's tromping in the woods, like as not for some herbs to spice up you kids' homecoming supper."

"You sure about that, Sheriff?" asked Eva, who didn't look as if she was ready to believe so easily.

Adam said, "Erica Wheeler is the law, and she knows. Anyway you got no cause to worry, Eva. I'm here. You're not alone."

Eva stood straighter now. "I ain't worrying. Aunt Viv says G-Mama tromps the woods like an Indian. I know she's just out tromping the woods."

"I know it, too," said Erica Wheeler. "Your uncles used to worry themselves sick about her going off all the time alone. That's why they got together and had that telephone line brought out here so them and me could check on her. I often thought it was a waste of good money. Every time we've worried and checked, we was the ones left feeling foolish."

Adam pushed against the old-fashioned netting of mosquito bar on the back door and went inside again. Eva and Erica followed. Adam sat down on the woven-bottom chair next to the telephone. "We'll wait her out," he said.

Erica picked up the phone and put it to her ear and then put it down again. "It's working, and that's what I ought to be doing. You call me as soon as she gets in and let me talk to her. If she ain't got back within the hour I'll be right back out here to pick you up. But I ain't worried about that."

55

Erica left, and right away time got heavy. Adam studied the black velvet picture of a stag that hung on the far wall. He'd never seen a stag in his life, but it looked like a strong creature that could handle itself in most any situation. Eva began walking around and around in the little front room, from cot to couch to rocker and back again. It made Adam nervous.

"Set down. I could be out looking and calling, if you wasn't such a baby about staying alone. One of us needs to wait here for her to come back. You'd only have to stay alone for a few minutes."

"I had another nightmare last night at the orphan asylum. It was a big scary-looking toad. I was out in the garden with my real mama and she made me go sit on a rock, except the rock was a big toad that jumped and got me tangled in its big hairy legs."

"Well, you ain't in no orphan asylum anymore. Anyway toads don't have hairy legs, Eva."

"This one did."

"See? That proves it was only a dream and nothing to worry about right now. Real toads don't have hairy legs. You're in G-Mama's house and her bed is so high that a real toad, even, couldn't make it on top. So you better just relax and forget about dreams. There ain't nothing you can do about what you dream anyway, except forget it. Now is it all right for me to leave to look for G-Mama?"

"Little Adam, the time wouldn't go so slow for us while we're waiting if we finished G-Mama's darning and mending for her. It always takes forever to mend a sock. Okay?" Eva dumped the contents of the mending basket out onto the linoleum floor of the living room.

It looked like he wasn't going to get Eva to stay in the house while he went out to call and search, so he might as well humor her. "Show me what to do and I'll do it." He pulled from the pile of mending a long black sock with holes at the toe, heel and knee.

He refused to put G-Mama's little brass thimble on as Eva insisted he do, for his fingers were tough enough to sew without the use of a thimble. He was cooperating otherwise, but Eva hadn't even learned him how to weave a hole shut in the knee of the sock when the phone rang. "Hello. Yes, this is Little Adam. G-Mama? Just a minute." It was Erica Wheeler calling, wanting to speak to G-Mama. He ought to have been preparing himself for such a call that was surely to come instead of darning some darned old sock. "It's the sheriff wanting to speak to G-Mama," he told Eva.

Eva's face went absolutely pale. "She'll come and get us. We'll end up in jail or have to go back to the orphan asylum."

"G-Mama's where she cain't speak on the phone right now," he said to Erica on the phone.

"You tell her to drop what she's doing, that I want to talk to her." Erica snapped out the command.

Snapping orders on the phone wasn't such a hard

57

thing to do. Lots easier than in person. "G-Mama's where she cain't speak on the phone right now," Adam snapped back.

"You kids is getting as sassy as she is. Is everything all right?"

"Everything's all right. I already had to darn some holes in one of her stockings."

A roar of laughter filled the phone until Adam had to move it away from his ear and then right back again to hear her next words. "I guess everything is all right there. Well, tell G-Mama the law says she's not to overwork you kids, and that I'll call again to-morrow when her hands ain't so full."

Adam hung up the phone and turned to an accusing stare. "You lied to a sheriff, Little Adam," Eva said.

"No, I didn't lie. It's what Uncle Windy would call a legal loophole. And she made it herself. You want me to call her back and tell her G-Mama ain't here yet and get us sent back to the orphan asylum?"

"Oh, no!" gasped Eva. "Little Adam, I keep thinking about Honcie, don't you? You think Honcie will ever get adopted? You think he'll have to stay there crying all his life?"

"Eva, don't talk like that! Look, I got Honcie to laugh about the turnip, didn't I? I got everyone to laugh. And if you laugh once in an orphan asylum, then it won't be so hard to find a way to laugh an-other time. Now think about that!"

"I'm thinking about G-Mama now and the fact that

it's getting dark. I think we ought to light a lamp."

Adam paused to figure how to tell Eva just what he was feeling. "G-Mama is causing us—me—plenty of worry by staying out this late when she ought to be here cooking a hot meal. I don't reckon I feel like lighting a lamp so she can just saunter on home slow and easy knowing we're here waiting. We'll wait until it's really dark before we light that lamp."

Adam often had had to wait for a thoughtless grown up who took an awful long time doing something. He had developed a fast way to fall asleep. He'd often used it to shorten the waiting time and soon someone would be waking him up and saying, "Let's go, boy." Now was the time to teach Eva.

"Eva," he said, "you ever get real anxious about wanting Christmas morning to get here?" He saw a look of disbelief come to her face. "I ain't changing the subject. Uncle Windy always said that the fastest way to make Christmas come was to go to sleep in a hurry. Well, I know a way to go to sleep real fast. Why I can fall asleep anyplace, whether it's behind a warm heating stove, under a wagon seat, or even sitting up between Uncle Windy's knees. Even when there's lots of loud talking going on all around me. You want to try it, Eva? Then first thing we know here'll come G-Mama waking us up and scolding us and . . ."

"I have nightmares when I sleep. Anyway, I'm hungry."

Eva! Always thinking of food. "Well, look in the

food safe and see if there's any leftovers. I'll go look in the cellar for a can of something."

The cellar smelled of the familiar roots rotting and sprouting. It still held over some of last winter's cold, but mostly it held beautiful rows of canned fruits and greens. He chose some red pears that looked almost purple in their blue Ball jar. He had had these before at G-Mama's at Christmastime, and knew they tasted of cinnamon. Eva had found some cold biscuits and had set out a speckled blue metal pitcher of milk. She'd made them both a couple of radish sandwiches. She ate hers faster than he did. He was in no hurry now, for he liked the coolness of milk from the tin cup, but Eva gulped her milk and then drank up the leftover juice from the pears too. She said, "Okay, now show me how to go to sleep fast."

"Fine. I will. I'll take the cot in the living room, and you take G-Mama's big bed."

"No. We'll both lay down on G-Mama's big bed; that way she cain't go to bed without waking at least one of us up first."

"Good thinking!" said Adam. "Now get real comfortable. Now think of your toes wiggling in sand. Now think of your legs just soaking up the sun in the cotton patch, feeling cozy and sleepy. Now think of your whole body lazy and resting. Now think of your arms feeling heavy and not wanting to move." Adam let his words come out soft and easy just as he always said them inside his mind when he did this trick.

60

Maybe he did or maybe he didn't get to the part of letting one's mind think about nothing; he'd never know, for Eva woke him screaming. A big hairy-legged spider was hanging just above her head.

"The toad! The monster! Get it away!"

"Eva, this ain't no nightmare. This is a real spider and I got him!"

Eva pulled the bedspread tight under her chin. "It ain't dark yet. Oh, Little Adam, I hear something."

Looked like he'd better find some words to mollify her. "That ain't nothing to be afraid of. That sound's a . . . *a morning dove!* Hey, where's G-Mama? It ain't night, it's morning! We slept all night and G-Mama ain't back yet. No one tromps the woods all night. You fix us some breakfast while I go looking."

"I ain't hungry, Little Adam. I'm coming with you to look. If I stayed here, I'd be setting on pins and needles wondering. I'll go."

"You're always hungry. Someone has got to stay here."

"Why? Two can look better than one. I got good hearing. Aunt Viv says I always hear things I got no business. I maybe could hear her calling. I'm coming along. You cain't make me stay."

He didn't waste any more time on trying to make her stay at the cabin. When Eva made up her mind, then that was that. She'd learned that much from Aunt Viv.

One nice thing about falling asleep with all your

61

clothes on was that you didn't have to waste time getting dressed. "Well, come on. Which way we going to start?"

"On a path, I reckon. People usually follow paths," Eva said, and it sounded like a fair statement.

They took the widest path that led out from the little barnyard. The sky was carpeted over with the soft gray clouds of early morning, and the cow was mooing, her udder hanging heavy with milk. The chickens pecked wildly in the dew-heavy grass and the pigs made their greedy racket. It was a temptation to stop to feed them, but if Eva could wait to eat, so could they. "We'll take care of you guys dreckly!" he shouted, and he loped on to catch up with Eva.

"G-Mama! G-Mama!" he called and they stood to listen.

"G-Mama! G-Mama!" Eva called and they stood still to listen again. All that could be heard was the movement in the bush of small animals or the scolding of birds. So it went with them walking down the path and taking turns shouting. Maybe they took a hundred, maybe a hundred fifty steps between calls. But their calls proved not worth a farthing; no one answered. Then suddenly Eva stopped short after no more than twenty steps.

"You hear something? You hear G-Mama?"

"It's not what I hear, it's what I see. Look!"

There a few yards ahead of them, stretched right

straight across their path, was a big old black snake. Eva turned back and began breaking off a branch. Adam put out his hand to stop her. "Leave it alone, Eva. It's just a black snake. Won't do no harm. Them snakes is a farmer's friend."

"Friend? A black snake will steal birds' eggs! Aunt Viv caught one gobbling up some little blue robin's eggs. They sure was cute little eggs. I'd been watching the nest for days, waiting to see the little birds peck their way out of the shells. Then woosh! That black snake finished them off. Aunt Viv grabbed it by the tail and flung it into the pasture."

Before Adam could clear his throat for a good logical statement in the black snake's defense, Eva had it by the tail and had thrown it far away from the path. Adam watched as it wiggled its way into safety among the tall squirrel grasses and green cattails by a little pond; then he said what he'd meant to say all along. "Leave nature alone. No snake and no animal and no person is perfect, and that one little fault don't make a black snake bad. Let the birds find out its fault and guard themselves. The martins do. It's a fact: a martin won't build in a tree with rough bark because of snakes crawling up."

Chances are, Eva never caught one word he'd said, and that made Adam mad. How was he going to learn her anything if she didn't stop gawking at the snake and listen. Then it hit him exactly what Eva had done; she had grabbed a snake and thrown it. "How

63

come you can grab a snake with your bare hands, and you scream wild fits if a spider comes near you?"

"No snake ever bit me, but a spider did once. I swelled up real big. My ankle was as big as a fruit jar and you could see it throbbing. I was little then and thought my heart had actually gone down into my ankle. I just don't want it to happen again."

Adam shook his head. There was no use wasting his breath trying to reason with her. Maybe if he'd lived around as many snakes as she had . . . Uncle Burl and Aunt Viv used to always talk of snakes.

Uncle Burl would roll out a big-chested laugh and say, "G-Mama's macaroni is fair, but Viv makes noodles out of copperheads, throws on a little tomato, and, yum!"

Aunt Viv would follow without laughter in her voice. "It's a fact that we cain't step outside without a thousand copperheads snipping at our heels. We got more than any other place in Missouri."

It sure seemed odd that Eva's nightmares weren't about snakes. Maybe dreams are caused by other things. He stomped on a bit of rotten bark, exploding a stinky puffball. "Let's find G-Mama."

That was easier said than done. They must have called a million and a half times until the woods rang with their voices, and the birds scolded and scolded, and Eva at last admitted that she was hungry after all.

Adam was getting downright worried about G-

Mama, and somehow that fact made him even more aggravated at Eva. He motioned for her to follow him on the path back towards the house. He was bone tired, tired of searching and of Eva's tagging on. Now where was his plan of getting Eva adopted and taken care of by a loving grown-up? Drat it.

"Look here, Eva, I'm going to feed the livestock and you can make us some breakfast. We got to manage things."

She gave him no sass. She'd better not.

When he got the chores done and went in for breakfast he found the rest of the biscuits and a jar of cold green beans. "Green beans for breakfast?" he screamed.

"Spiders are in that cellar. I got what was closest to the door." Eva dumped some beans onto his plate.

"At least you could have heated them up. Cain't you make a fire?"

"You sound like Uncle Burl. Spiders was on the woodpile too. The beans ain't raw, just cold."

Now this spider business had gone too far. Adam stalked over to the pile of wood by the kitchen stove and sure enough there was a fair-sized black spider spinning its web from the cold stove down to the pile of wood. He made a swipe for it and fell and skinned his shin. It smarted like heck but he didn't cry. And he didn't scream mad so as to have Eva call him Uncle Burl again. He laughed and laughed until tears came.

"Eva, see that crazy swipe I took? Won't that make a right funny thing to tell G-Mama? Here, give me them cold beans. Won't G-Mama think that's a funny breakfast when we tell her? Won't she just die laughing?"

Eva had her mouth full of beans, and Adam knew she was trying to act proper and not talk with her mouth full, but he kept nudging her until she managed a green smile. That was more like it. Uncle Windy would have approved. He helped her polish off the whole quart of green beans and then said, "Come on, there's lots of paths in the woods. We better get moving."

So again, they walked and called and listened. They didn't make more than five or six listening stops, and hadn't left more than a quarter mile between them and the cabin when Eva said, "Quiet! Quiet! Listen."

"You hear G-Mama?"

"No, but I hear something. It's this way." Eva shot off to the right of the path, never even noticing the big spider web that she split right down the middle as she ran. Now Adam could hear the sound too. It was a dog whining, or his name wasn't Adam. He got his direction and outran Eva right to the spot.

"G-Mama!"

There she was lying flat on the ground, her hair unrolled from its bun, her dress twisted tight beneath her, and next to her was a little skinny tan puppy running round and around, whining for all he was worth.

"What took you so long? I been out here all night! I expected more than that out of you twins." Her voice got a little lower on the last words and the puppy got louder. G-Mama was fighting off any help to lift her up, so Adam picked up the puppy instead and got him quiet.

Eva reached over to a small clump of grass and picked up G-Mama's bonnet and handed it to her. "What are we going to do, G-Mama, if we cain't move you?"

"I didn't say that you cain't move me. Naturally I'll have to get back to the house. I'm hoping this is nothing more than a bad pulled muscle causing this pain, but if Ericky finds out she'll think for sure my hip is busted. Then she'll not be saying that you kids can stay on. What she don't know ain't going to hurt her none. Anyhow, I'm glad to see you two got back safe from Saint Louis, and I'm glad you found me."

"G-Mama, me and Eva will make a pack saddle with our hands gripping our arms tight and you can *ride* back to your house."

"If I could sit, I wouldn't be laying here, would I?"

Adam understood G-Mama needing to sass, so he went on. "We could make a pack out of our clothes and have you home laying down all the way."

"Too soft. Not meaning no offense but I'm sending one of you for help, and the help is got to be some-

67

one who can keep their mouth shut. Adam, follow this narrow path straight on to its finish, and you'll see a little two-room shanty in the clearing. That'll be Leatha's place. Tell her to come and to bring her linked cot springs. They'll be flat and sturdy."

Adam started to put the puppy down so he could take off running, but G-Mama said, "Take the pup with you. I think it belongs to Leatha's hound."

Eva said, "It's a nice pup. It saved your life, G-Mama. If I hadn't heard it a-barking, I'd have never found you. G-Mama, if your hip really is busted, it won't keep Erica Wheeler from letting you adopt us, will it?"

G-Mama said, "We cain't keep that pup if he's Leatha's. And as for this adoption business, it don't mean nothing. You're mine. They let you come back to me, didn't they? Anyway, I figure this is just a bad pulled muscle."

Adam figured G-Mama wasn't as sure as she was letting on and was just trying to comfort Eva. Well, she was going about it all wrong. "Adoptions mean a lot to some people, G-Mama. Pretty soon, when you get all well, we'll just go tell Sheriff Wheeler that you can too adopt Eva. You ain't too old. You'd only need eight more years and you're from sturdy stock. How's that for a legal loophole? Eva won't have no more worries. Right now though, we better not let no one know you're hurt. They won't let hurt people adopt. Even if your hip is busted, it won't take more'n six weeks for a bone to heal. I busted my arm once, and it healed in six weeks. We just got to lay low for six weeks."

He gave Eva and G-Mama a moment for that to soak in and added, "G-Mama, I better run and get your neighbor Leatha real fast. Sheriff Erica Wheeler said she'd call again today, and we better have you home in time to answer that phone when she does call."

six

Leatha lived in a shack with a rusty tin roof and lace curtains at the windows. She was a straight thin black woman, not curvy as Aunt Dory or G-Mama even. Just straight as a corncob with the same reddish fuzz of the cob for hair. Her face was pure in its lines and open to friendship. When Adam told her what G-Mama wished she'd bring for help, Leatha did not hesitate one minute to yank from her small daybed the network of tiny little springs all hooked together.

"I'm ashamed of myself for not hearing that little hound pup. But with four more in the litter, how am I going to know which yelps comes from where, or if one's missing?"

The pup ran along at Adam's heels all the way, as he and Leatha hurried back to the rescue. He made no effort to stop the pup but yelled ahead, "We're here, G-Mama. The pup come back too. Leatha's got four more."

"Welcome, Leatha. If you can spare that smart pup, I'll be pleased to take it. Put the springs right alongside me."

"G-Mama, you poor thing. You bad hurt? Now easy does it, just grip hold on my arm and sort of roll while I pull you. Lands, you got more than your share of bad luck. Lost your man after a scanty short marriage, raised all his boys, and now they all gone. Now bad luck's hit you directly."

"Leatha, nothing hits me directly. It may sneak in but I'll see it get ousted out. Oh-h-h-h, that smarts. Leatha, please, you carry the front end; Little Adam, you and Eva each grab a back corner of the frame. Lordy, it's hot out. I'm blinded by my own sweat."

For a second there, Adam thought Eva was refusing to carry her corner of their makeshift stretcher, for she was busy untwisting her handkerchief. But Eva wasn't dallying, she used the handkerchief to mop G-Mama's face, and used it again and again every time they had to set G-Mama down to rest a bit. Eva seemed to know more what to do with sick people than he, but that was all right, he'd learn. He had to.

When they got G-Mama to the house, Leatha and Eva probably never would have got G-Mama up on her high bed without his help and direction. And it was he who pulled the bed across the rag rug and close to the wall-phone. He was a good help but he demanded no thanks for it, for this was the way he wanted it. G-Mama did start thanking Leatha though, over and over again in sort of a feverish way. It seemed to be a mighty effort for G-Mama to stay awake and talk.

Adam whispered to Leatha, "You think she ought to see the doctor?"

"Doctor!" shouted G-Mama, alert as could be. "I've never been to a doctor in my life. It's a waste of money that poor people don't have in the first place. The earth provides enough to take care of its inhabitants. Never had to take any of my boys neither. God still watches over us. Don't let them kids keep you from your own chores, Leatha. Many a thanks I give you. Don't you worry about me. I still got my pep, though that moving onto the bed was a mite more pain than I could stand for a minute or two. I can use the kids here for my legs. We'll make out fine."

G-Mama was final in her order and Adam knew that Leatha would obey her and leave, but he hated to have Leatha go. It looked like it was going to be a long six weeks of laying low.

Leatha said, "You're welcome, you're surely welcome, G-Mama. Now you kids come outside with me and let your G-Mama rest."

As soon as they got outside, Adam asked, "What do you want to tell us that you don't want G-Mama to hear?"

"I tell you right this minute, she a sick lady. She won't give in to no doctor, but you keep your eyes open."

Eva said, "Maybe we could go in town and get her some patent medicine."

"No, that woman won't take no medicine, except she makes it herself. Now if she go too light on her food, or get the chills, you let me know. Nighttime comes, won't hurt none to keep a little fire going in the heater. She was expecting her boys to take down that heater for the summer, but then the accident come, and they done finished their good deeds for her. Poor woman got more than her share of trials. Remember now, if this turns out to be worse than she thinks, I'm right through the woods. You call whenever you feel the need."

G-Mama was calling. When they got to her bedside she asked, "Which of you can make a fire the fastest?"

Adam never gave Eva time to take her breath. He yelled, "Me," and made a dash for the kitchen stove. G-Mama's statement of "I could eat a bite" came like music. She hadn't gone off her food yet. That was good.

"I ain't afraid of spiders neither," he yelled for Eva's benefit, as he hunted for the little tin can that held kerosene-soaked corncobs to be used as a fire starter. He put in the cobs, threw in three sticks of ash stovewood, spiders and all, and struck a kitchen match to it. It caught. "The fire is started! Now what?"

He didn't know if anybody heard the question he'd called out, for that little scrawny pup was a-yelping and carrying on something at the back door. He walked in close to G-Mama and said, "If I don't let that pup come inside, nobody's going to be able to hear one thing in this house."

G-Mama smiled. "I never believed in house dogs before, but . . . nothing's too good for that pup. Let it in and give it a name."

The pup jumped in before the door got open two inches. "I tell you, G-Mama, he can get through the narrowest space of any pup I've ever seen."

Eva said, "He sure is a scrawny pup. Come here, Scrawny, and stay off G-Mama's bed."

"Now that the dog's named, we got other things to think of. Little Adam, can you milk?"

"I can."

"The cow is lowing. I imagine she's in pain. Take the pup out with you and do the milking. I cain't rest when I hear a creature in pain."

Scrawny would not go out the back door, so Eva whispered, "I'll keep him in the kitchen with me. Now hurry up with the milking."

It was nice of Eva to offer to keep Scrawny. If they both worked together, they'd manage. He hurried along as fast as he could and got the milking done. But when he brought the milk back for Eva to use in cooking, she didn't thank him.

"Scrawny cain't stay in the kitchen. I started to make G-Mama some pudding. When I turned my back to get the flour out of the flour bin, he ate my eggs and drank the top cream that I brought in from the milk house."

Problems! Family problems. Well, he'd have to face up to such, he guessed. He'd have to be a man like Uncle Windy and not buckle under. "G-Mama said there wasn't nothing too good for that pup. So put a smile on, Eva, and just be happy he didn't lap up the sugar too."

"Eva! Little Adam! Come in here!"

They both made tracks towards G-Mama. Scrawny came scurrying along in and around their feet all the way to the bedside.

"I've been resting and I've been thinking. You kids ain't very old, but you're all I got. I cain't move for the time being, and that's a fact, like it or not. I'll have needs of a private nature that will have to be met. Now listen close and I'll tell you how we'll manage my toilet, Eva. And, Adam, you go find me some cornstarch. It's setting on top of the warming closet. The sweat from all this heat has me galled. Maybe it serves its purpose; the irritating gall does serve to keep my mind off the constant ache in my hip."

Adam started to look for the cornstarch so G-Mama could powder her gall, but she snapped, "Isaiah 6 : 5."

"What? What you want, G-Mama? You want the Bible?"

"I want you to get the Bible right over there and look up Isaiah 6 : 5."

"Right now? Before I get your cornstarch?"

"Right now."

He got it and read, " 'Woe *is* me! for I am undone.' " Boy, G-Mama sure had a fancy way of complaining. But there she lay, laughing and pointing at the open fly of his pants. He turned his back and, quick as a thought, buttoned himself to decency. He couldn't bring himself to laugh along with her and Eva. Still he appreciated the fact that G-Mama practiced the same ways as Uncle Windy of laughing the hardest when things looked the worse.

Her laughter stopped and her face grew pained and serious. Eva stopped her laughter in sympathy. G-Mama said, "Kids, there is a place for modesty, and then there is a place where it is properly forgotten. A sickbed is one of them places. I want you to accept that. I bathed and cared for your little bodies when you were newborn. I hate to have to say it, but now your turn has come."

Adam knew it was going against her very nature to have to ask favors, and she needed to justify having to do so. "We're glad you took care of us, ain't we, Eva? And it sure is our turn to pay you back and we're glad to do it, ain't we, Eva?"

Eva stood nodding and a fine delicate smile came over G-Mama's pained face as she continued. "What a sight you twins was! Eva, you weighed three pounds two ounces, and Little Adam, you weighed three pounds five ounces. Everyone said you'd die, but I knowed you wouldn't."

"We're not going to let you die neither, G-Mama," whispered Adam.

"Of course you ain't! But I'll have to tell you what to do. Have to give you orders like I gave them orders: 'Don't change these babies' clothes every day, for they're too weak to warm themselves; and don't pick them twins up unless it's to feed them. Let them rest and sleep.' That's what I ordered, and you lived!"

"We won't make you move or make you change clothes," Eva promised. "We'll do whatever you order."

"Now it took you a few years to catch up on growth, but you made it, and it may take me a spell too, since things don't go so fast at the beginning or ending of life."

Adam knew this was true. Uncle Windy use to laugh and say, "You didn't weigh no more than twenty-seven pounds, clothes and all, when I packed you off to first grade. Man, I hated to let that little mite go off into that big old schoolhouse."

Adam looked at G-Mama, who looked just a little mite of a thing stretched flat under that big nobby chenille spread. He whispered again, "You'll make it too, G-Mama. I growed like sixty once I started school. We'll be patient. We ain't babies anymore. We ain't worried about a thing, are we, Eva?"

The phone rang and Adam handed it to G-Mama to

answer. He was certain who it was calling. G-Mama sounded sprite as anything as she answered Sheriff Erica Wheeler with, "I'm fine. Managing fine with the kids. Thanks for hauling them out. Sorry I wasn't here right on the minute. You do that, Ericky, call again."

It was plain lucky that the sheriff didn't wait a day or two later to make that call, for G-Mama seemed to get weaker as the days and nights passed. Adam wasn't sure if he was getting weaker or stronger from all the chores he was having to do. He would come in from milking or chopping wood, wash his face to freshen up and cool off, grab the biscuits and green onions Eva had out and ask, "Is G-Mama off her food yet?"

Eva would answer, "I guess she eats it all, I never find no leavings." But Adam caught the glance Eva gave towards Scrawny. Scrawny was putting on weight at a most unusual speed.

Eva was more than worried about G-Mama; she was scared too, for herself. This was plain to see, for she was twisting her handkerchiefs to the point of wearing them out. Here Adam was in a house with a fat pup, a sick woman and a scared girl. The pup seemed happy enough, and if Adam was any sort of a man at all, he'd have the other two viewing life the same way. All they needed was some reason to laugh to cheer them right out of all this gloom.

So Adam told G-Mama just how funny everything

had been at the orphan asylum. He told how he had been the first person to get blood from a turnip. Like a good storyteller, he laughed loudly and laid it on thicker than it actually was until he made G-Mama laugh too.

Eva interrupted him to say, "Adam, you're as bad as our uncles. You make everything that has happened seem fun. Why is it that fun is always in the past?"

G-Mama said, "Let him be. When he talks, I forget the pain like as if it was Windy talking."

Adam directed most of his talk from then on to G-Mama, since it was no use trying to get Eva to see when a thing was funny when she had her mind set wrong to commence with. Sometimes all the work and worry and Eva not helping matters any sort of got to him. He got awfully tempted to go fetch Leatha. But that was dumb thinking. Leatha surely thought by now that all was well, and as long as she thought that, there was less chance of G-Mama's condition leaking out to Erica Wheeler. That would get him and Eva into more trouble than he cared to imagine. So he just stuck in there and waited and worked and laughed and hoped.

Then one day G-Mama called to him when Eva was out busy gathering a batch of roasting ears. He knew something was wrong when he saw the look on G-Mama's face.

"Little Adam, I don't think I'm going to mend.

This hip of mine ain't setting just right. Now listen to me, son. You come from good stock. Your granddaddy once set Burl's ankle which got throwed out while clearing new ground. That ankle mended fine and never gave Burl a minute's trouble. Windy once lanced a bone felon for me. My thumb was swollen to a strut, and it was turning black and throbbing until it was impossible for me to think of anything else, just like right now. I told Windy to take the straight razor and lance it. He sure hated to, but he never once said, 'I won't.' He went white when he done it but he laid this thumb open with one sharp cut. The poisons spilled out and the throbbing stopped. After that it was simply a matter of healing." G-Mama showed him the scar.

Adam knew where all this telling was leading. A great fear filled his muscles until they became immovable.

"In my day, I've set many a bone. Not just my own boys' but a little neighbor girl's break that was near the elbow—and once a black woman's hip. I got a feel for bones. All you got to do is follow exactly what I say. Exactly. Now, Little Adam, grab hold my right leg."

He obeyed. He was more scared now than he'd ever been in his life, but his hands reached out and he got hold of G-Mama's leg at the ankle.

"Put your hands just a few inches up. There, there. Now raise the leg. There, that's enough. Now

80

a bit to the right, no . . . drop it a little. There! JERK!"

He obeyed! He obeyed! Something moved and G-Mama screamed. He let her leg down easy and stood sobbing. Eva came running in screaming, "What happened? What happened?" Scrawny was chewing at Adam's pants legs and snarling furious snarls.

G-Mama looked white and dead. Scrawny began to howl.

Adam's hands went flying toward the telephone but then he heard a whisper. It sounded like, "Thanks, Little Adam."

He grabbed up Scrawny and patted him on the little white spot on his rear. "Now hush! You'll upset G-Mama. She's been through enough for one day."

Scrawny shut up enough so that he heard G-Mama's next soft command. "Little Adam, go to Kirkwood's store and get me a half pound of flaxseed. You tell him I said, 'Charge it.' Eva, get some water hot so we can make a poultice."

Eva asked, "What does a poultice do to help, G-Mama?"

"Don't ask G-Mama questions. Just do what you're told!" Adam scolded.

"Let her be," said G-Mama. "You kids are free to ask any question you want in my house. God gave you mouths for saying more than just yes, right, Adam?"

"Yes," said Adam. And he grabbed Scrawny and

started to leave, hesitating only a minute when he heard G-Mama saying, "Eva, in case I should faint again . . ."

Scrawny ran on ahead as if he knew where the store lay. Adam heard the cry of a quail and whirring wings of the mother and her brood that the puppy caught unaware. Smoke was just beginning to curl over housetops, meaning neighbors were starting supper. And from all these people he must keep a secret. He'd have to watch his words at the store.

He walked right into the store and quickly stated his needs. "My G-Mama wants a half pound of flaxseed and she said to tell you to charge it."

"G-Mama wants a half pound of flaxseed and charge it, you say? You're one of the twins. Orphan twins. She ailing?" Mr. Kirkwood talked as he reached for one of the little bags all neatly tied with store string.

He had a strong look of curiosity about him, so Adam quickly said, "She just sent me to get flaxseed, because I wanted to go out with my dog. Yes, she says charge it." With that said, Adam grabbed the bag and yelled to his pup, "Here, Scrawny," and took off.

He ran as fast as if the devil were chasing him, and indeed he was sure of it. He'd sat at Uncle Windy's feet and watched the faces of storytellers and the listeners of stories and he knew, he just knew what people were thinking at times. He figured that Mr.

Kirkwood would come out checking on G-Mama. As much as he hoped that he had guessed wrong, he was sure he'd guessed right.

Mr. Kirkwood arrived at the door of G-Mama's place at four o'clock that afternoon. He had on his red shirt, the one with its pocket worn thin from carrying a snuff tin. His hair was spruced heavy with oil and parted on the side, which let thin strands of hair partially hide his bald spot. He came through the door, pushing Eva aside with his walking cane, and walked right on in to G-Mama's bedside.

Adam thought to be polite and offer him a chair, but he had already seated himself in the split-bottom rocker and was leaning forward. Never did lean back and use the chair as it was meant to be used. He was too set on talking. "You must be pretty sick, old woman, sending a boy to do a man's job. That boy couldn't keep your secret if *his* life depended on it. Now what ails you and why you hiding the fact?"

Adam was furious. The nerve of that old man to barge into G-Mama's bedroom and start badmouthing people. Saying he'd given away a secret, which was a downright lie.

"G-Mama fainted. She can faint all she wants to, and she don't have to tell the whole world about it."

"Little boy, I'm seventy-six years old. That's not yesterday I was born. Tell me how to get you to see reason and I'll try it. Flaxseed is either used for a laxative or a poultice, and you don't need a half pound

83

for a laxative. G-Mama ain't charged a thing for five years, and that was when she couldn't find where she'd hid her cash. I figured she was down with a sprain or a break, and at her age it'd most likely be a hip. I twisted my leg once. That's what got me this cane. Well, old lady?"

Eva said, "G-Mama ain't an old lady."

"Well, well, the other little freckle-face is speaking. Look, I don't care if you both are smart-aleck snot-nosed orphans that's out trying to protect your G-Mama. I want answers from her, not sass from you. Children ought to be seen, not heard! G-Mama, you tongue-tied?"

"Kirkwood, I won't have you saying things to upset my grandchildren. These kids always got a right to be heard in my house. But I ain't afraid to answer your questions, *old man*. Yes, I did do my hip in. But it's been set and I figured I was mending. With the flaxseed poultice, I'd be doing fine, that's what I thought, until you come in shouting."

"Why all the secret? Why cain't you ask a man for help?"

"She's adopting us, that's why, old man. Cain't you use *your* head?" That was Eva! That was scared little Eva bawling out Mr. Kirkwood. Boy, Eva sure wanted to get adopted; so much it made her bold enough to stand up and speak out.

G-Mama said, "Now Eva, don't be baited by all this talk. I don't like you saying things that's disre-

84

spectful to Mr. Kirkwood. I'll tan your hide soon's I'm up and about if you do it again. He come as any good neighbor would, I reckon."

"And as a good neighbor, I'll tell you that a poke-root poultice beats a flaxseed poultice anytime for fast healing if it's near a joint. What's this about you meaning to adopt these kids? Ericky could never persuade the county judge to draw up papers for you to do that. You're a single woman!" Mr. Kirkwood paused for effect.

Well, Adam was sure affected by what he'd heard. What good is there in hearing a new fact that pulls your hopes right out from under you? He'd already thought up a fine loophole of how he was going to outtalk any judge objecting to G-Mama's age. Now what good would it do him to explain that G-Mama only needed to live for eight more years to raise them full-grown, and that she could do that hands down because she was of a stock of people that always lived to near a hundred? Now it'd take a loophole and a half to convince a judge that G-Mama wasn't single! Adam really felt pained. By the looks on G-Mama's and Eva's faces, he guessed they did too.

"Course, I could fix that little problem for you in a hurry. Tell you what—if that hip of yours mends, and you don't have to use a cane, I might consider marrying you." Mr. Kirkwood's mouth never ceased smiling and his hands caressed the rocking-chair arms.

G-Mama tried to throw her pillow at him, but Eva

held her down. "I wouldn't marry you, Kirkwood, if you was . . ."

"I told my grown daughters to stop trying to dissuade me from marrying you. I asked them if any of them was willing to come live in my house, cook for me, wash my clothes, help out with the chores. That stopped their arguing. Now that we got them agreeing, and that took me ten years, all we got to do is get you well. Better give pokeroot a try."

He paused, waiting for G-Mama to comment, but she didn't. Then Mr. Kirkwood must have taken that for a good sign, for he leaned even farther forward in the rocker and said, "I'm a considerate man and a patient one. My life was half spent before I lost patience with my first wife. She was so tight she'd boil down gnats to make lard. I'd rather, the geese be eating grass off my grave than have to live with another one like her."

Eva scooted over close to Adam and whispered, "I don't believe that his dead wife was all that bad."

"Course not, sh-h-h-h," Adam whispered back. He figured Mr. Kirkwood was just about run down and his motor would shut off soon enough if they didn't give him any extra fuel to go on.

"What's that the girl said?" Mr. Kirkwood was twisting his head around like a sunflower trying to pick up every little comment.

G-Mama said, "Sniffle-snort, Kirkwood, it don't matter what her words was, she just don't believe any of yours, that's all. She probably was thinking that no woman could be as bad as you let on. Eva don't talk much, but the girl's got plenty of pluck and don't swallow all the air she's exposed to. Why, any child knows that even a broken timepiece is right at least twice a day. You cain't fool my kids nor me with your talk."

"Well, old woman, you'd best listen to what I have to say. Pokeroot could've had you up and around already."

"I'll give the flax time to work. If it don't, I've a mind to try mustard plaster next. I been doctoring as many years as you can remember, Kirkwood. I don't need your advice or your credit either, if it don't come willingly. I still got the good Lord."

"Where was He when you got that hip messed up?"

"The Lord don't spare you from the rain, He just helps you manage when you get caught in it. He moves mysterious. You know that. Little Adam, bring Kirkwood something to snack on."

Adam got two cold biscuits and some yellow pear tomato preserves and set them out before Mr. Kirkwood. Eva brought him a cup of herb tea, which he filled half up with sugar that refused to dissolve. He sat relaxed now and G-Mama seemed relaxed too, just as if she had enjoyed all this bickering and talk-swapping.

G-Mama was a smart one, all right. She was surely

trying to get Mr. Kirkwood in a fine mood so he wouldn't go away mad and call Erica Wheeler out of spite. Well, why not get his spirits really high. He said, "Pokeroot might work as a remedy, G-Mama. It's commonplace enough. Uncle Windy said it cured his itch once, and Aunt Dory declared she could cure anything with pokeroot juice if it was boiled strong and dark and not watered down."

Mr. Kirkwood smiled at the help Adam was giving his side of the argument. "Like I was saying, it'll sure work. I was trying to crank my car and got my arm broke. My mammy set it and we applied pokeroot poultices and it healed up dandy." He rolled his arm around in front of them for their admiration, then got up and announced, "I'd best be leaving."

The back door was standing ajar and Mr. Kirkwood started to leave by it. Adam didn't want him snooping to find any unfinished chores, so he followed closely. He bumped right into the old man when he stopped suddenly and pointed toward the porch rafters.

"Now there's a fine walking cane if I ever saw one. I could use a new cane that's got something to notice on it. You ought to see the one Mr. Silts showed me the other day. You wouldn't reckon you could speak to G-Mama about. . ."

"He'll not speak to me about that cane!" shouted G-Mama. "I'll thank you to not pester me again about it."

Mr. Kirkwood left at once without another word said. Adam hoped G-Mama hadn't undone all that buttering-up. Hoped that Mr. Kirkwood remembered the best part of his visit and not the last and would choose to keep his mouth shut.

Adam felt the situation was as fragile as a row of dominoes sitting on ends, where one little wrong move, just one little slip of the lip, and all his hopes would come tumbling down. If Erica Wheeler should happen to find out, she'd most likely just haul them back to that orphan asylum. She'd say they needed to be taken care of, instead of trying to take care of G-Mama.

Well, he didn't call living at an orphan asylum being taken care of. It took a real home, and that was what Eva was going to have, by golly. He'd get her adopted proper like he set out to do. He didn't know just how they would be able to keep Mr. Kirkwood quiet. He'd just have to be prepared for the worst. If G-Mama got discovered before her six weeks' healing time was up, then he'd just have to take Eva and make a run for it.

They'd have to take along G-Mama's gun so they could live off squirrels and rabbits. He could manage. He'd manage until G-Mama got all the healing time in the world that it took, then he'd come back and let her adopt Eva. He wouldn't let her being a single woman foul up things. He'd thought of a way past her being too old, so he could also think of a way past her

89

being single too, if he thought hard enough. He sure didn't want to have to think of G-Mama marrying Mr. Kirkwood. It was a good thing that man owned a store, with all the sugar he took in his tea.

Adam's ears were whistling from all that thought zipping around in his head. But whatever *was* he thinking? He'd just let himself get stuck in what seemed a bright clear center to his thinking when he ought to have looked to the edges, where the thoughts were hazy. When he used clear thinking all the way through, he knew he couldn't run off to save Eva. That would mean leaving G-Mama alone with no one to care for her.

seven

When Adam was out doing yard chores, caring for
the livestock or working in the garden, even playing
with Scrawny, he always had one eye out for the road
to see if Sheriff Erica Wheeler's truck was heading
their way. So far it seemed that Mr. Kirkwood hadn't
let go their secret.

Adam and Scrawny had just finished one long
happy run and were coming puffing in through the
back door. Neither G-Mama nor Eva heard them
come in, for the two of them were going at it.
G-Mama had been ornery ever since she gave up on
the flaxseed poultice and tried a mustard plaster and
blistered her skin good. Before he left for the run this
morning, he himself had mixed up a bunch of sulfur
and lard for her, and Eva probably hadn't put it on to
suit her. Nope, that wasn't it. G-Mama was yelling
something about rhubarb!

"So! Them rhubarb roots I give to Viv didn't rot in the ground like she claimed! Who cares if the leaves are poison, nobody in their right minds eats 'em. I tell you I need rhubarb for my system to cut down on this itching. Just bring in some stalks and make the pie like I told you."

"A-hem, ahem, ahem!" Adam gave a good warning as he walked in on their quarrel. It was hard to believe that Eva, who never had dared give Aunt Viv sass, was being free as Mr. Kirkwood with it now.

Eva said, "G-Mama, I got the pie dough rolled out and that took me a million hours and I want to fill it with something else besides rhubarb. I don't want to make a pie and not get to take one bit because it's poison. It's too much work."

Eva was exaggerating about the million hours of course and he would have called her on it except he felt sorry for her. "Come on, Eva, I'll help you. Aunt Dory had me cut her rhubarb for pie all the time. I can do it fast as a flash."

Eva was fast herself in leaving G-Mama and joining him to go to the garden. G-Mama yelled, "Little Adam, I had in mind for you to cut me some broom straws and make me a little body scratcher when you got in."

"I will directly," he called back to G-Mama, "but don't you know a little pokeroot juice would have that itch cured in no time?"

"Little Adam, you're a-pumping me for a fight and I ain't having one. Now git!"

He and Eva got out in a hurry and had a whole bundle of rhubarb stalks cut and in a pile before their breath had settled to a normal flow. "Now what?" asked Eva. "You ever see Aunt Dory make a rhubarb pie?"

"Sure, lots of times, but right now Scrawny needs a hat." He took one of the big rhubarb leaves and made a hat for his hound and said, "That's a reward for being a good rabbit hound." He made an even finer one to fit his own head, and then he looked towards Eva and she smiled and stood waiting.

"They ain't poison or you wouldn't be handling them, would you? If they was really poison like Aunt Viv says, you wouldn't have put one on Scrawny, would you? You love your dog and you wouldn't ever hurt him, would you?"

"Course not, Eva. That's a dumb question."

"Aunt Viv believed they was poison even to the touch and she wouldn't plant the roots G-Mama sent home with Uncle Burl. She hid them out behind the barn and let them rot."

"Why didn't she just tell Uncle Burl so's he could plant them himself or give them to someone else who might want them? That was wasteful."

"Now *you're* dumb, Little Adam! If you throw away poison, then that ain't wasteful. Anyway, she couldn't tell Uncle Burl 'cause it ain't proper for a woman to disagree with a man right to his face."

That did it! For a whole minute Little Adam stopped his work on the two big rhubarb leaves he

93

was busy twisting together. "If that be the case, Eva, why are you disagreeing with me right to my face?"

"Because I ain't a woman yet—just like you ain't a man."

"That's silly. Absolutely silly." He realized, of course, that Eva wasn't a woman and that she was a child who needed adopting but . . . Well, it looked like Eva was getting in the habit of running off at the mouth. Talking entirely too much. He finished attaching the stems of the two small leaves he held and draped them over Eva's head, one dangling on either side. He'd learn her a lesson.

"That's not a hat, Little Adam. I want a better hat than that."

"No. No, don't take them off. Leave them on a minute. We're going to play a game. First you got to promise that you'll say the same sentence I do except I'll end mine with *lock* and you end yours with *key*. Okay? I'm a tin lock. Now you say 'I'm a tin key.' Go ahead."

"I'm a tin key."

"I'm a gold lock."

"I'm a gold key," said Eva right away.

"I'm a silver lock."

"I'm a silver key. This is a silly game. When does it end?"

"I'm a don lock," said Adam without pause.

"I'm a donkey," said Eva, and her face went blank for a second and then broke out in fireworks.

Little Adam pointed at her dangling rhubarb ears and, quickly grabbing up the bundle of rhubarb stalks, ran towards the house shouting, "Eva is a donkey. Eva is a donkey." Scrawny yipped at his heels and, with Eva's shouting, it all made one glorious racket. They stopped at the back stoop and sat down to rest from all the hard laughing. Obviously, Eva hadn't learned any lesson, but she sure was having fun.

Eva said, "Little Adam, we're together."

"Of course we're together, and I mean us to stay that way."

"Are you sure we can?"

"Sure, I'm sure. I can lick anything I set out to. I can even lick the law if I have to!"

Eva didn't smart anything back. Instead, she chose to just sit and look at him for a while. She looked pretty tacky herself with the drooping rhubarb ears and her dress torn and pinned shut with a big safety pin. She hadn't had time to sew it what with making poultices and cooking and all.

"Here, I'll show you what size Aunt Dory cuts these stalks soon as I get them washed." He held them in a bundle and sliced off the entire lot of stalks one inch at a time. Then he scooped up the short pieces and threw them into the pie crust Eva had ready. "There, now put some sugar on."

"How much, Little Adam?"

He grabbed a handful of sugar and sprinkled it

95

around like he'd seen Aunt Dory do so often. He wondered if Aunt Dory made it to Texas okay and if she got that job cleaning. Maybe he ought to get one of G-Mama's postcards from her nightstand and write Aunt Dory.

He said, "There! I ain't helping you no more." Then he added, "Aunt Dory puts flour in for thickening too."

He walked away from Eva because he had to. He was overflowing with loneliness. He hated running the world with a twin. It would be good right now just to have any man open that door and hail him and let him know that he was in a world of grown-ups. Oh, Uncle Windy, why do you have to be dead?

The door swung open and Mr. Kirkwood quipped, "Howdy, Little Adam. Howdy, Eva. How's G-Mama fairing? Thought I'd check."

Adam had hoped for someone to come through that door sort of like Uncle Windy. Mr. Kirkwood was sort of like a pain that refused to stay away. It didn't appear that G-Mama needed any more fights today to raise her spirits, so Adam said, "G-Mama's fine. She's sleeping, I think."

"I ain't sleeping!" called G-Mama from her room. "Bring Kirkwood on in, Little Adam, and Eva, you hurry that pie along so's we can share."

Adam thought better of it but he obeyed G-Mama. Right off, Mr. Kirkwood proved Adam's judgment sound by saying, "G-Mama, you're looking right peaked. Got to get well if you aim to marry *me*. Your garden ain't doing so good either. Tomatoes has got the limberneck. Looks like a bunch of geese out there with their heads a-bobbing. The sweet potatoes has sprouted your tub full and the slips ought to have been set out, at latest, a week ago."

G-Mama was trying to hide her feelings with a smile, but it didn't work. Adam guessed she was still trying to keep on Kirkwood's good side. She pushed up on one arm a bit and said, "Little Adam, ain't you been working the garden?"

"I'll say he ain't!" Mr. Kirkwood's voice was full of tacks as he continued. "These kids been pulling turnips for you? I could get a couple neighbors in and have things set straight in a minute."

Little Adam cut in fast. "You cain't have neighbors in! We cain't let it out about G-Mama being down, you know that. You been telling around?"

"Now get down off your high horse, sonny, or I might have second thoughts on leaving you here with an ailing woman. As for keeping secrets, I can as good as the next one. I ain't told a soul yet, but I might if your G-Mama don't give in and say she'll marry me."

That was too much for G-Mama. She shouted, "Kirkwood, you're pressing well over the line. I don't need a husband; I had a husband. You go opening your mouth, and word leaks out to Ericky, you can consider this the last time for a visit in my house."

97

"Now, G-Mama, cain't you take a little joking? Maybe I talk a little bit but we all got our faults; no one excepting. Even that husband of yours had faults too."

Little Adam was ready to come to G-Mama's aid, for he knew that only good was allowed to be said about Granddaddy. But G-Mama wasn't rankled at all; she was settling back on her pillow with a smile on her face. "I reckon he had one fault. I told him that our marriage wasn't a deal if he didn't shave that mustache of his off. I cain't abide a mustache on a man."

Adam said, "I can. Uncle Windy had a fine mustache and I'm going to have myself a fine mustache when I grow up."

"Windy never had no mustache when he was home with me; he got it after he married Dory."

Eva came to join the talk. "The pie's in the oven. Uncle Windy didn't have any whiskers enough to have a mustache when he was home, did he, G-Mama?"

"Eva, you do better to stay near your pie and watch it. Well, when your granddaddy showed up the day before our wedding still wearing that mustache and claiming he always would, I fed him and let him nap as was his custom. Then I took the candle from the dinner table and, figuring to singe it just a little so's he'd have to cut it off, I set it on fire. He woke up fast enough and had it out, but he couldn't shave the rest of it off proper for a week, for it blistered his lip. We never had no wedding pictures taken."

With hardly a pause, Mr. Kirkwood asked, "Wonder if Ericky will take a liking to Furnet's mustache. Yessiree, he's back in town sporting a red mustache and asking around about Ericky. Lost his wife, the man did. A man needs a wife. It's a fact. Hold down there, G-Mama. I ain't bringing up the subject to rile you again. I'm leaving. Still think I ought to get a neighbor or two to come over and give you a helping hand. I'd offer myself, but every time I even come calling, I got to close down the store, and that's no way to do business."

Adam followed Mr. Kirkwood outside to ask the question that last speech of his had called for. "You tell this Mr. Furnet about G-Mama? You better answer me true!"

"Me and Furnet was too busy talking about him moving back into the house he's been letting out to Leatha to talk of much else."

"You better not tell. We need to get them adoption papers bad, and I ain't having anyone ruin the chances for that."

"A boy your age whining to be adopted. You ought to be ashamed! Why, you ought to be acting like a man and . . ."

"It ain't me, it's my sister, Eva, that needs adopting, and she's got good reasons. I'm going to fix it so's no one can give her away again. I can take care of my own self."

Mr. Kirkwood slapped Adam a few bony pats on the back. "That's the spirit. I know how it is with girls, though. My girls is all growed now and none of them worth a dime. Many's the time I'd like to have given them away but, the fact be known, you couldn't a-hired me to do it. They was mine, such as they were. Yes indeedy-deed, we got to look after our womenfolk. Your uncles looking after G-Mama was what kept her saying no to me all these years. But now that they've passed on, she'll soon be missing all that loving care, and . . ."

"I can take care of G-Mama just fine. We don't need no help with the garden either. Give me two days and you'll see!"

"Thataboy, spoken like a man. You take care of that garden and I'll take care of her other needs. She's likely to run low on cash soon if she ain't already. All women got to turn to us men when the going gets tough. Look at Leatha. She had to go home to her pa now that Hank Furnet needs his house back. And her pa took her in even though he has thirteen others in his house. That's the way it is, boy." With a jaunty little flick of his cane, Mr. Kirkwood left.

It certainly left Adam with plenty to chew on. Leatha had seemed content there in her little house with her pups. It was a shame she had to leave just because the owner popped up out of nowhere and said he was moving back in. Maybe she'd be a help in her pa's house. She sure was a helpful woman. Adam guessed he'd banked awfully heavy on her being there to help out with G-Mama if things got to be more than he could handle.

And what was this about Mr. Furnet wanting to marry Erica Wheeler? He didn't know what to think on that subject but he'd best put it aside as something important enough to remember. For some reason Adam thought that right now might be a good time to take Scrawny for a run, maybe through the woods over toward what had been Leatha's place.

eight

Being the man of the house, Adam wouldn't dream of causing G-Mama any worry by leaving without first letting her know that he was taking Scrawny for a run in the woods.

She gave him no thanks for his doing it. "Don't mention woods. Here I am drowsy as a setting hen but fighting off napping. The last time I napped, I dreamed I was running naked in the woods. I've always heard that dreaming of a naked woman means a person will die. I feel like a trapped animal fighting off my sleep like this, but I've had enough!"

"I wouldn't believe all that stuff about dreams if I was you. Your mind is getting lazy when you start thinking of things like that to worry about. Best you exercise your mind by hunting up finer things to think about. Uncle Win—"

"I need exercise, all right. I need to get my sifter of ashes and go out and take care of them cabbage worms Eva told me about. I need to get out and cut a rank of wood. Eva says we're getting low. I'm weary of this bed. I'm weary of sickness. I'm weary of being helpless."

Adam snapped, "Eva talks too much." He searched for something cheering to say. "Did you notice how, when everybody was talking, Scrawny kept up with the highs and lows with his growling and whining? There, don't that help your spirits just a little to think on that?"

"Maybe a little. But . . . I ain't one to be laid up. I want to see my garden. I want to see what you been doing and I want to give a word of advice."

"You think we could move you into a chair and let you set by the side window?" Adam suggested, feeling strongly his manly responsibility of caring for G-Mama's needs in some manner.

"I may be giving in to telling my wants, but I ain't took leave of my senses. Use your head, Little Adam. A busted hip ain't a busted leg."

"Well, right from where you're laying you can look out this window here a little, and see them two feisty little squirrels running up and down the elm," said Adam.

G-Mama raised herself to take a peek and then lay flat in bed again with a sigh. "I'd love to shoot one of 'em. Chances are the other one would get away, but we'd have us a fine batch of squirrel, stewed tender. I can taste it. I love to kill squirrels. Deer, too. I shot a bobcat once, too, before the lumbermen cleared up so many woods they all left the country. We don't see wild animals around like we use to have."

"Rabbits is wild. I told you I need to take Scrawny for a run in the woods. We just may come back with a rabbit. I'll teach him to catch it himself. You'll see."

"Gr-r-r-r!" Scrawny was pulling away at the fringe on G-Mama's bedspread.

"See, I told you he could do it. He's getting anxious to get out and stretch his legs. We'll see you when we get back, G-Mama. Maybe we'll have that rabbit. You think on that. Eva, you keep an eye on G-Mama. Where'd Eva go?" Now how could a man give orders if half his family disappeared on him?

Adam didn't have to look far, for Eva was out in the garden pulling turnips like mad. "Why are you doing that? I wanted you to stay with G-Mama for a while."

"Mr. Kirkwood said we ought to be pulling turnips for G-Mama."

"Drat it, Eva, you don't have to obey everyone that yells at you. No one's going to beat you if we don't. Now get back in with G-Mama. I'll pull them turnips later."

"I don't think you will, Little Adam, but I'll go in."

At long last, it was time to let Scrawny run, and it just so happened that Adam's legs got stretched a bit, too, trying to keep up. Scrawny picked up full speed and was howling so that it could only mean one thing. The real hound in him had picked up the scent of a rabbit. Faster and faster they went, dodging branches and logs, on and on until they came to the clearing of Leatha's former place.

Adam stopped. That must be Hank Furnet pumping water. He was a fine big man with deep brown skin and sandy hair and whooping fine red mustache. He sure did need a woman, for buttons were missing from his shirt, and strong muscles and chest hair showed through. Bet no one had nightmares or bad dreams in that man's house. So this was Sheriff Erica Wheeler's beau. Now to see how Leatha was faring.

Another good run, and he and Scrawny were at Leatha's pa's place. Lots of faces looked out at him and then Leatha's voice called out, "Little Adam? Your G-Mama all right?"

Adam waited until she came out and stood near him to answer, "G-Mama's fine, just fine. I been taking care of her. We only got three people in G-Mama's house. You sure got lots in your family."

"I have for a fact. You got some idea of wanting to even out the score? G-Mama send for me?"

"If you need a place to go, if you're sort of crowded being here with your pa, well, I'd be pleased to have you keep G-Mama and Eva company. G-Mama is weary with loneliness."

"I see. No point in her being lonely. You just stand

105

here and talk dogs with my brothers and I'll go round up some clothes."

The boys asked what kind of dog Scrawny was, and Adam told them hound—one of Leatha's pack of pups now playing in this yard.

Leatha came out with a bundle of clothes, and they made haste right back to G-Mama's house. Adam called as he opened the screen door to come in, "G-Mama, I didn't get no rabbit. I got Leatha. She didn't need to be cooped up with all her pa's family. She wanted to come, didn't you, Leatha?"

"For a fact, G-Mama. How you doing? I notice the garden as we come by. You need a helping hand."

G-Mama and Eva were all mixed up with surprise and pleasure. G-Mama finally gave up trying to sort it out and said, "Leatha, I need my legs most, but next to that I welcome your helping hands. First thing I'd like to ask you to do is show Eva how much sugar to put on rhubarb. That's the sourest pie I ever ate. Guess the acid will do some good though, for my stomach."

Adam said, "As long as you're teaching Eva, well, Eva says it don't make no difference to the stomach if a potato is cold or hot. But it makes a big difference to my mouth, and I wish you'd tell her that potatoes ought to always be hot."

Leatha laughed. "Ain't you ever heard of cold potato salat, child? Come tomorrow, if you two help me get that garden in respectable shape before dinner,

I'll make you some. You won't never complain about potatoes being cold again. Right now I got more important things to do."

Leatha opened her bundle and took out some red nail polish and painted G-Mama's fingernails. Smiles started bursting out one by one until finally there wasn't a long face left in the room. Then came the laughter which made Adam feel right at home. He didn't even mind sleeping on a pallet that night; it was worth it having Leatha in the house.

The next day Leatha and Eva had the house chores done by the time Adam had finished milking Jersey. Leatha asked, "You ever ash cabbages before?"

"Sure, sure I know how," Adam answered, which wasn't exactly a lie, for he had seen Aunt Dory do it, and he was almost double positive he could do it himself. But that old sifter of G-Mama's worked mighty funny, and Leatha took it from him after a few struggles.

"Flick this little wire here over to the left, okay?"

"Okay," said Adam. "I was just fixing to do that very thing."

Next she tried to teach him how to transplant the sweet potato slips when he already knew how. He gave up on that part of it and settled for using the lister plow to throw up the rows for the potatoes. He worked and he worked and Leatha could surely see that he turned out almost as much work as two grown men. His palms had blisters on them right under the thumb, where it is impossible to tie a rag around it and make it hold in place, but he was man enough not to complain.

G-Mama had rung the bell that Leatha had hooked up for a signal, and Eva had gone in to care for her needs, but Adam and Leatha worked on.

"If the season lasts long enough, these sweet potatoes may just make something yet. Never hurts to try," sang out Leatha.

"Never hurts to try," sang back Adam. And he realized suddenly that he was being happy working, just like when he was alongside Uncle Windy. Strange, but he hadn't thought of Uncle Windy all day. "How long you going to stay with us?" he asked her.

"You asking that because you want me to leave or want me to stay? I working you too hard?"

"Heck, no. I can take all you ask. You're welcome to stay as long as you want. I mean that."

"Well, I reckon I might stay around until Mr. Furnet finishes his stay or gets married or something, and lets me have my little house back once more. Unless you chase me off before then."

"Mr. Furnet going back to Illinois right away?"

"I don't reckon right away. Says he's been considering this, that and the other but ain't settled on anything yet. The man is sick to heart and overburdened at his own sorrow at being without a wife. Both his girls are married now. I think myself he's come back here to get Ericky to give up being sheriff. That's a dreamer thinking, for that's the very thing that busted them up the first time."

Adam listened carefully. He needed to learn everything he could about Erica and Mr. Furnet. Who knew what might be useful?

A slight sound made Scrawny sprint in pursuit of a rabbit that came shooting out across the garden. "Get 'im, Scrawny. Hound him down, boy!"

Leatha went right on talking. "It worries me a bit what might happen if Ericky says no to him again. Mr. Furnet can be an angry man if things don't go his way. They ain't a thing angrier than a white man when he hits hard times."

"I ain't angry," said Adam.

"I didn't say you was a man. Well, it don't pay none for Mr. Furnet nor any man to get mad at what is, like it don't pay me none to stand here worrying. My daddy has had his share too, but he waste no time on worrying; he tells me to watch the poplars. They bend and take the wind, and soon as the wind dies down they stand straight again. You hear a word I say, boy?"

"I hear you, Leatha. I'm pulling turnips."

"I see you are, Little Adam. I see you worrying some too. How about me and you both keeping watch on the poplars? I ain't leaving you for a while yet, don't you worry about that."

"I ain't worrying about that. I was frowning be-

109

cause G-Mama likes to make soup out of the sprouts from the turnip hills but the days are hot and the sprouts has all rotted away. She'll have to settle for fresh turnips."

"She'll settle. I'll stew 'em up fine and throw in enough red peppers to give 'em taste and give her a cleaning out. She'll need that, being bed-bound."

Adam did not answer nor did he show any signs for Leatha to see that he was a bit embarrassed. Her talking like that just proved that she felt like one of the family with free and easy speech. It was almost like Leatha was family and it was good, for Eva had found it easy to talk back and forth to Leatha just as she was doing with G-Mama and Adam.

It seemed even more like Leatha was family as the days wore on. When they got back inside the house, G-Mama was being careful to let her nail polish dry. Eva had painted G-Mama's toenails, too, since she had to stay barefoot in bed. Eva met them bubbling with laughter and telling them how she had also pulled three long hairs from G-Mama's chin.

"Eva, ain't it bad enough to have a busted hip without you having to go jerking hairs out of her? I said you should cheer her up. I didn't say . . . Now stop it, Eva, this is no laughing matter!"

"Shut up, Little Adam!" G-Mama ordered as she rubbed her chin. "You was the one that got her to laugh. Besides, it feels good to have them pesky little hairs gone. Listen here, Little Adam, you better be quiet or I'll hold you down and have Eva jerk the hairs out of your nose."

He knew that G-Mama was just bluffing. She didn't have enough strength of her own to hold down a feather tick, but she felt new strength in having Leatha around and was back to being her old self again. Everybody sensed it the same, for Leatha chuckled and Eva was smiling. Adam's vision got blurred with tears in spite of himself. It was fine having everybody so happy again.

Eva said, "Mind if I pick your guitar for a while, G-Mama? They say I take after my daddy. I pick real good." Eva got the guitar down from its nail, tuned it up, and started strumming. She sang "Home on the Range." Leatha joined in the singing. It sounded really nice. Little Adam could neither pick nor sing, and it just seemed to be the wrong time to do something that he was good at . . . He couldn't for the moment put his finger on just what he was good at.

"Come on, Little Adam, sing!" sang out Eva.

"Eva, leave me be. I'm tired. Tired as a hired hand. I did too pull them turnips like I said I would do."

There was pressure in back of his eyes again, and it was not coming from being so happy. Look, wasn't it him what got Leatha over here to start all this singing and stuff? Being the man of the house was an awfully important thing, and they'd all better give notice to that fact.

111

G-Mama sighed and said, "This strumming and singing reminds me of when my boys was home. I miss having a man around the house."

"You got a man around the house!" Adam stalked out the door.

He went to the toilet and sat there watching an inchworm inch its way across a Sears Catalog page. People had to be like that sometimes, taking things inch by inch.

Well, he might as well chop some wood. That was man's work, and he figured he could handle it. G-Mama had some big tree limbs laying out in back that could be sawed into cookstove length and then split. Her crosscut saw pulled heavy. Must be too old and worn. He got four lengths sawed off though, and then picked up the ax.

Wham, whop, whack. No girl could chop wood like that.

It was late in the day and the shadows were long. The shadow of the little cedar was a good five feet long. Aunt Dory said if you let a cedar tree grow big enough to shadow your grave, you'll die. He thought of G-Mama and her dream. He was the only man around here, and he sure wasn't going to die! Quickly he took his ax to the cedar and chopped it into pieces!

Scrawny was barking and jumping around in the midst of the cut cedar branches. Adam gave him a few fanning strokes with a branch, thinking he wanted to play. Then he saw what Scrawny was really barking about. He had brought up a dead rabbit! "Great boy, Scrawny. You can do it. I knew you could." Adam looked at the rabbit laying to one side of the cedar branches, stretched its full length, laid out like an offering. He accepted it.

Adam picked up a load of cedar stovewood pieces and held them with one arm and chin; with his free hand he carried the rabbit. When he got back inside that house he was going to speak out like a man and let the women appreciate just who he was around this place.

He dropped the wood with a mighty thud beside the cookstove and shouted, "You women going to cook G-Mama up a good supper or not? Eva, there's wood aplenty to make your fire. Leatha, you know how to cook rabbit?"

Leatha was up by a high cupboard cleaning, and Eva was helping and they were both still singing. Leatha stopped her scrubbing and said, "You say something down there, Little Adam? It'll take a good lot of wood to fry rabbit. Where'd you get that fine rabbit?"

"I managed. There's plenty more wood where this come from. Now you two can let that job go and get some supper made."

They laughed and, contrariwise, finished their song. " 'Nothing could be finer than to be in Carolina. . . .' " Eva sang with such gusto that Adam

113

hadn't the heart to point out that this was Missouri. It wouldn't have rhymed anyway. Gosh dang, that Eva was looking about as happy as if she were already adopted. She wasn't even hungry as usual, else she'd be more interested in getting that rabbit cooked. Lot of good it did to act manly around this house.

The next morning Eva had even a happier look, if that was possible. Added to all that fun and laughter now was the look of achievement. Adam knew she was going to tell him about it, so he didn't waste her time by asking questions. But she said the darndest thing when she did speak. "I had that monster come back and visit me in a nightmare again last night."

She paused to wait for questions, and Adam almost satisfied her by asking one too. He was curious but he knew she'd tell soon enough without him giving in and asking why.

Eva said, "It was the same giant green toad with the red fiery tongue and hairy legs. But I got rid of him once and for all!"

"I hope you did, Eva, but don't bank on it. You cain't ever do a thing about what you dream."

"I can and I did."

She didn't go on. She was getting almost as good at telling things as he was. She sure learned fast. "Okay, so what did you do, Eva?"

"Well, Adam, you said you could lick anything you set your mind to. I'm your twin so I set my mind. I just told that monster to play 'tin key' with me. At first he didn't do anything but look mean and croak and that was scary. Then he started to talk back to me and played the game and when he was the donkey he began to hee-haw and to laugh and shake. All the shadows got shook away and it wasn't a monster no more and it wasn't ugly. It turned out to be my real mama. She had on a pretty green dress with a red scarf about her neck. She said to me, 'Eva, honey, don't be afraid anymore. I'd a-stayed and took care of you if I could. It was an accident. You're a big girl now and doing real good at caring for yourself. You're not with Aunt Viv. You're with Little Adam and G-Mama and Leatha. Everything's going to be all right.' And I know it will too. I ain't afraid."

Adam didn't feel like arguing any point. He'd just have to see to it that Eva stayed happy like this so that nightmare never did come back. And any man who can run a house, work a garden, and provide wood and wild game can surely get a sister adopted proper and legal and keep her smiling all the time.

nine

Adam figured his muscles had grown a good half inch a week since Leatha had come. He'd sure managed to get a great amount of hard work done around the place. Plus his usual milking and wood chopping, he'd done any other chore that Leatha wanted help with. He was beginning to let her teach him a few things.

G-Mama would ring her bell and one of them would run to get her a dipper of water or whatever. At these times, Adam would also ask her something about her life with Granddaddy just to keep her spirits up. She sure delighted in telling of the time when she had wiped Granddaddy's face with a wet dishrag or of the time she'd powdered his hair with flour or of the time she'd wrestled him in the snow. "Oh-h-h-h," she'd delight to the memory. "He was a strong one. All I could do to handle that man."

Adam wanted her to be happy again like in the old days. Maybe when she got well she could find herself another fine man like Granddaddy. Not Kirkwood, but a strong, good man like Uncle Windy, a man like Adam wanted to be someday. At least such a marriage would get rid of one problem, her being single. But it'd take a really strong man, for problems were mounting in spite of everything, and Adam was feeling the fact that he was only ten years old.

For four weeks Kirkwood had not squealed to the sheriff, which left only two more weeks until G-Mama's healing time was up. Erica Wheeler had telephoned a couple times, and G-Mama had pretended to be hale and hearty when in fact she wasn't at all. Leatha seemed concerned about G-Mama's lack of progress, and had taken to helping Eva change the poultices each day. On one of these times G-Mama said, "You're sneaking a new poultice in on me. What is it?"

"It's smashed pokeroot. That's the best when you been hurt near a joint," explained Leatha.

"Where'd you hear that? Kirkwood?" G-Mama demanded.

Adam figured he'd better step in and help out. "G-Mama, you want to get well, give it a try."

Eva's hands trembled as she placed the poultice gently over the hip. Her face hung sad and hope was all gone from her voice when she added, "You cain't adopt me if you don't get well, G-Mama."

"All right," said G-Mama. "I'll try your old

pokeroot, providing Adam cooperates with me on what I ask. Eva, get me my scissors. Adam, you sit down beside this bed right now. It's been a long time since I cut anyone's hair, but be thankful I ain't singeing it off with a candle."

"I'll go to the barber in Bernie," Adam said quickly. "Give me the money, and I'll walk over there right now."

"We got no money," G-Mama said. "No cash at all. Now get down there."

Adam sat still. He was so shocked by G-Mama saying they had no money that he didn't dare to open his mouth to speak. Anyway, he'd probably get hairs in it. Scrawny was already rolling around in the hair that fell from the scissors. Adam picked up some hair between his thumb and finger and put it up to his upper lip like a mustache. Maybe there was something to hair giving strength like it said in the Bible. It seemed that just about all the really fine strong men that Adam knew had a mustache. But he was only ten, and he wouldn't have a mustache for a long time.

Leatha took the last couple of snips off Adam's hair because G-Mama just had to lie back flat. She groaned and then demanded, "Well, somebody say something. I know you're worried. But we'll manage. I've sold roots and berries and mushrooms to stretch out the cash my boys used to bring over when they came to visit. I could go ahead and apply for old-age

118

pension so's these kids could have schooling, but I'd
have to see Ericky to do it and I don't dare get ahold
of her until I'm well."

Adam said, "Me and Scrawny could spend more
time hunting. And I can pick cotton. I been picking
cotton for two years now."

"Cotton. There's the answer. These two kids could
pick enough to get their winter clothes. Every little
bit helps. Leatha, I know you and your family picks
for the Pearsons every year. Would you go over and
ask if they can include us too, this year?"

"I sure will. I'll trot over right now and ask."

G-Mama went on planning. "I ought to be healed,
and up and around myself, by cotton-picking time.
There's the Silts' place next to the Pearsons', Leatha.
Ask him if we can get picking there, too. I don't like
the man personally, for he married a good Pentecos-
tal woman right after her husband died and squan-
dered her money on himself. They say he bought
fourteen walking canes. I don't believe in old folks
marrying; causes nothing but talk and hard feelings."

Well, didn't look like G-Mama would solve the
adoption problem by finding another fine husband
like Granddaddy. Looked like Adam better pull all
the strength he could from himself for a long haul at
picking cotton.

Eva said, "Cotton-picking time is a long way off
and we need sugar for canning right now."

Adam said, "The other day Scrawny was stalking

119

mice round the ditch dump, and I swear one of them animals was no mouse. It was big. I think it was a muskrat. I've fixed what I think is a good trap and I'll sell animal furs."

"Walking canes. That's it."

"What's it? You talking about Mr. Silts?"

"Never mind, Adam. When you do go down by the ditch, try a little seining. I got a seine and I love fish better'n cake any day. There's lots of good eating in them ditches. We'll manage fair enough. We'll have to get things to a pattern right soon before Leatha's place is empty again, and she gets to go back to her own garden and chores. I've always managed and I've lived through some pretty hard times. Once when we couldn't sell our corn, we picked it anyway and used it for stovewood. Parched corn tastes mighty good too. Maybe I'll be up and around to help with the heaviest part of the canning. Berries must be getting ripe. A ten-year-old girl ought not to have to can by herself. Lands, I'm weary of this bed."

Adam said, "Eva won't have to do it herself. I'm here, ain't I?"

Eva said, "I'm sure glad you offered, Little Adam, for there's spiders and webs in some of them empty jars out in the cellar way. I want you to wash them. I still cain't take to real spiders."

"Look," said Leatha, "if Little Adam could go get the sugar right now and charge it while I'm getting things settled about cotton-picking jobs, then I ex-

pect tomorrow would be free for berry picking and canning."

Adam knew that G-Mama would be set against charging anything more with Mr. Kirkwood so as to become beholding to him. He'd best just ask her how much and make a dash for it before she had time to get riled. "How many pounds, G-Mama?"

Without hesitating, G-Mama said, "Twenty-five pounds will be enough for you to carry home, and that will do for canning this week. But I ain't taking credit. That cane's still up on the porch rafter; take that. A lumberman found it out growing like that natural, and he brought it to me as a present. Kirkwood's coveted it for a long time."

Adam found the beautiful wooden cane with its different shadings and interesting knots. He and Eva examined it. Eva said, "You might want this for yourself when you get up and around. It sure is pretty, G-Mama."

"Never! If I need a cane, I don't need to live."

Adam took the cane and went hobbling down the road on it. He used it to clear his path as he hobbled on over to the ditch to see if he'd caught anything in his trap. Hey, where was his trap? Oh, there it was out in the water. He used the crook of the cane to pull it back in. It must have been a pretty big muskrat to have slipped that sliding door and dumped his trap in the ditch. He'd best make his trap a little stronger if he was going to sell pelts. If he'd had a nice big coon or muskrat right now, he'd have been able to save G-Mama's nice cane. He wiped the cane on his pants and went on to the store.

He handed the cane over to Mr. Kirkwood without fanfare and asked, "This cane worth the price of twenty-five pounds of sugar?"

Mr. Kirkwood stood staring and acted as if he didn't hear or wasn't interested.

So, to stir up a friendly response, Adam said, "G-Mama's trying the pokeroot."

At that Mr. Kirkwood ordered, "Pick up that fifty-pound sack there and load it into my truck."

Then Mr. Kirkwood hung G-Mama's cane over his arm and grabbed a gray felt hat. He set it far back on his head as if to look younger than he was and headed out to the truck. He stopped to tell a man that he was closing to go visit G-Mama, who was ailing. Little Adam groaned inside himself when he saw the man was Mr. Furnet! Suppose he thought it was his neighborly duty to come calling, and then told Erica Wheeler what he found.

Adam first frowned at Mr. Kirkwood and then, getting a better thought, gave him a wink and said, "Aw, there's no need for fuss. What G-Mama's got ain't so bad, just awfully contagious."

Mr. Furnet left without comment. Mr. Kirkwood hung out his CLOSED sign, and with the use of his own cane hobbled out to his truck. Adam rode with him back to G-Mama's. G-Mama wasn't going to like it! He'd get one good scolding for letting Mr. Kirk-wood haul him back with fifty pounds of sugar. But how was he to fight a full-grown man? One with two walking canes?

Adam obeyed the old man's orders even up to tak-ing the bag of sugar in and setting it down by G-Mama's bed. By the time Mr. Kirkwood got in there too, G-Mama was already ranting and scolding, for she'd spied the truck from her window view.

Mr. Kirkwood didn't hold back on words any longer. "I got no time to waste. I'm getting old, old woman, so hear me out. After my first went, I could have got myself a younger wife, but I didn't want any more young'uns."

Mr. Kirkwood took a deep breath but went quickly on. "I still ain't wanting any more young'uns of my own, but I know that you're attached to these two and they could come along if they mind well. Now I own a store. I ain't broke. You could stop worrying about food money."

It had been pretty silent while Mr. Kirkwood sounded off, but the minute he stopped, G-Mama opened up. "Kirkwood, I cain't abide a scoundrel who'd take advantage when another is down. I'm trading with you but what I'm swapping is not myself but a walking stick which you been hankering for! You don't want to swap, I'll sell it to old man Silts and buy my sugar with the cash."

Kirkwood's voice came back without edge, but the

words showed the sharpness. "Now say all you want, but first I'd like to remind you that you're laying flat on your back when you say them words. Your airs don't fool me. I knowed sooner or later you'd start needing to lean on a man, now that your boys has passed on. I welcome your leaning on me for advice. That pokeroot will have you healed in no time and we can get on with the wedding. So, I ain't charging you for the sugar and I ain't taking your walking stick until you give it to me as a wedding present."

"You trade for that sugar! And you either change your line of talk or you leave my house this minute!"

Eva stood silently by, looking scared. Then she started singing, and Adam knew that she was trying hard to drown out the commotion.

Adam put his foot down hard on the tip of the empty rocker and set it into motion. "Say, wasn't that Mr. Furnet I saw down at your store?"

The unexpected change of subject made Mr. Kirkwood appear as pleased as a rabbit that had just spotted a break in the fence. "It was Furnet, all right. So you recognized him? Got sharp eyes just like me. I knowed him the minute I saw him, in spite of his new mustache. Did you know he took this course to be a highway patrol up in Illinois and passed it? Yep, now he's a real cop. He's likely to marry Ericky and then take over the job of being sheriff himself."

Adam let them go on discussing the probabilities of such while he figured out what that might mean.

124

Mr. Furnet would make a fine sheriff. He was a big strong man, but he would be less trouble for G-Mama to handle than Erica Wheeler. She'd managed a whole lumber camp full of big strong men for years. She'd have no trouble getting him to get the adoption papers. But, in the meantime, they would need money.

Adam interrupted their talk of Furnet to ask, "Could I sell you some berries if we get extra? I'd let you have them for ten cents a gallon." When Mr. Kirkwood nodded, more plans to make cash money for his family just leapt into his head. "My dog catches rabbits. You wouldn't be in the market for some good frying rabbits, would you?"

Mr. Kirkwood nodded again. "Yep, and I'd pay you a fair price for them too. I heard that pup of yours. With that bay he's developing, I'd expect him to be good for possums or coons, too. Just bring anything you catch around to me. Your G-Mama . . ."

"Kirkwood! Don't turn the subject back to me. I think you ought to leave now because I need my rest."

She jerked the covers up under her chin and turned her back as far as the pain would allow her. Mr. Kirkwood got up to leave.

"Mind if I ride back with you?" Adam asked. "I need to go to the mailbox."

In the box, he found a postcard from Aunt Dory. In very tiny writing it said:

125

Dear Little Adam and all,

I'm working steady. Weldon lost his job and is coming to join us as soon as I get his train fare to him. I wish you was coming too, Little Adam. One of these days.

There's cactus down here that blooms. I haven't seen any cowboys yet. It's dry and hot. How's your garden, G-Mama? I bet the berries is ripe.

Well, you all be good. You too, Eva. I hear Viv is settled all right in California.

Love, Aunt Dory

Adam took the card in and read it out loud to G-Mama and Eva. Eva said, "Gee, I guess you're an orphan just like me, Little Adam. Aunt Dory ain't ever going to come back or send for you."

G-Mama said, "You better do the milking."

Adam got a pan of water and took it out to clean the cow's udder before milking her. He tripped over Scrawny, causing him to dump the water all over the pup. Scrawny went whining and running away, and he was still making plenty of racket as Adam washed the cow's udder with the remaining bit of water. Too much racket from one little old water splashing! Adam went to investigate.

Something swooped past him overhead. It was a buzzard sailing in to get one of G-Mama's chickens. Adam grabbed a dead branch from the pile of firewood. The buzzard didn't like his interfering and was coming in awfully close to Adam's hair. He wanted to drop the branch and run. Scrawny barked unfailingly. That buzzard could make off with a pup as well as a chicken.

Adam beat harder and harder at the buzzard and his heart within him beat harder and harder with fear that the buzzard might win. He couldn't let it. Finally the buzzard was the one that gave up and flew away. Adam grabbed Scrawny and then sat down to rest and to quieten his dog.

Was that the kind of protector his Grandaddy, Uncle Windy and all great men of strength were? It was sure something worth pondering and telling, too, when the time was right. For the present he put Scrawny aside and set himself down on the milking stool and put his head to the Jersey's flank and slowly began milking.

Swish, swish, swish, went the steady stream of milk against the inside of his milk pail. *H-m-m-m, h-m-m-m, h-m-m-m,* came a steady little hum from . . . why it was Leatha humming. And she had a huge muscular man standing beside her. "Leatha, I didn't hear you come up."

"I know you didn't. Now I hope you can hear what I'm about to say. We got jobs. All of us that can work. Meet Mr. Jones." She stopped for a moment and even in the growing darkness he could see her beaming with pride. "I always heard that Mr. Jones was a mighty man but I didn't expect to find him *overseeing* Mr. Silts' place." She paused again to smile and Mr. Jones smiled too but said not a word. Leatha continued, "Thanks, Mr. Jones, for seeing me home through the dark. We'll come over soon's the first cotton opens. Little Adam, you know Mr. Jones can pick two hundred pounds of cotton a day?"

"I think you're stretching things, Leatha. And it ain't dark out yet either."

Mr. Jones smiled again and said, "That's a feisty little hound dog you got, boy. Hold on to him so he don't follow me off the place."

"He won't follow. He never leaves my side unless it's to chase wild animals. My dog is real good at catching rabbits; and I ain't stretching the truth when I say that."

Adam practically hollered the last words, for already Mr. Jones was taking long strides on the path back towards the Silts' place.

"He sure don't need none of Mr. Silts' walking sticks, does he, Leatha?"

"No, that man don't need nothing but a good wife. Now I wasn't stretching the truth one bit when I was praising that man. He has become a legend among us. Every farmer around feels honored to have him pick in their cotton patch, and they let him do things his own way."

"No one's got a way to pick two hundred pounds in one day. That's impossible."

"For Mr. Jones it's possible. First, he be the kind

of man that can hold still in a windstorm, who's not fearful of nature. Early in the morning when the world is still wrapped in darkness and the cotton is at its heaviest filled with dew, he chooses to start his day. He picks from that moment until the last ray of sunlight is lost to the horizon. He never leaves the fields, not even to eat. Part of his bargain as a hired hand is that he be supplied with eight biscuits and a large Clabber Girl baking powder can filled with navy beans to be delivered to him every four hours on the spot. And if he ain't picking, he ask a dollar twenty-five a day. No one's refused him yet. That be part of any man's strength, to not be afraid to say how much he's worth."

Leatha started humming, and Adam let the milking be for the time and followed her into the house. He shouted, "Hey, G-Mama, Eva, Leatha's back and she's got a beau who is giving us all jobs!"

G-Mama said, "Well, light a lamp so I can see who I'm talking to and tell me about it."

Leatha lit the lamp and, with her arms sort of wrapped around herself in a self-hug, crooned, "For years I've been concerning myself for the purpose of my life, and I've found it now in the need of Mr. Jones."

"Mr. Jones ain't got no need, Leatha. He's got the strength of three men, I bet."

"But what he's lacking is the strength of one woman to go along aside him."

"I got to finish the milking. I've started it two times already."

No one seemed to mind that he was leaving. Leatha was humming again and Eva had run to get the guitar. Even G-Mama looked happy.

Adam stopped at the door and demanded in a very deep voice, "I'd like some supper when I get in from my chores! I'd like some hot biscuits and enough navy beans to fill a Clabber Girl baking powder can, and maybe you'd better use that biggest iron skillet and pile it high with fried potatoes." He swaggered from the house as any man knowing his own worth has the right to do.

He swatted Jersey on the rump and said, "Move over a step. I never start a job I don't finish." He sat on the stool and began the rhythm of milking. He happened to notice how thin his pants stretched across his knees. Maybe if he earned enough picking cotton, he'd buy himself a new pair. The cow's udder was almost empty now, but Uncle Windy had taught him never to leave a cow without stripping the udder totally dry.

This he was doing when Eva burst through the barn gate shouting, "Erica Wheeler's come causing trouble! Get inside and help us, Little Adam!"

ten

Adam ran with his pail, slopping out half of the milk before he reached the house. As he entered, he heard G-Mama saying, "Ericky, you'll get a wart on your nose sticking it into other people's business which is of no concern of yours! I'm not going to be banished from my own home!"

Erica said, "G-Mama, I'm trying hard to be patient!"

Adam had to do what he could. He yelled, "Well, we don't appreciate your trying. What's G-Mama's business, she's got a right to tend to herself."

Erica let out a deep sigh. "G-Mama, I wish you'd understand that this is a matter for the law, and it is my business. I'm the sheriff."

"Wish in one hand and spit in the other and see which gets full the fastest," snapped G-Mama. "I ain't one to lose my temper but . . ."

"Oh, no? Well, from where I stand I'd say you was in a perfect rage right now. I can wait," said Erica.

Adam wasn't happy at all to hear G-Mama using sass like that, for it only meant that she had no more fuel left on her side. The sheriff could see right through all that smart-aleck talk. Besides, it didn't change Erica's mind a whit. She stood waiting. Adam figured he had better say something.

"It ain't against the law to get your hip busted, is it?"

"No, it ain't, Little Adam," said Erica Wheeler. "But if the law covers telling big whopping lies, I'd have to haul you in right now. For my own sense of mind, do you mind telling me why you told Hank Furnet that G-Mama was down with an awful contagious disease and couldn't be visited? You ought to have knowed that would bring me a-running."

Adam didn't have even a legal loophole to jump into. He'd best give his reason for lying and let it be. "We didn't want you to know that G-Mama was so bad off. We figured you might hold that against her and not let her adopt Eva. Eva needs adopting bad."

Eva said, "That's right. We was afraid you'd hold it against her. Adam didn't want no stranger like Mr. Furnet out spreading the word. I saw Mr. Furnet and he was asking questions about G-Mama, but I didn't say one solitary word back to him."

That statement of Eva's sort of threw Adam for a minute. "When did you see Mr. Furnet?" he asked.

"When you was getting the mail. I was picking

some berries. I wanted to be the first to bring some to G-Mama, and I was. I don't like Mr. Furnet. He reminds me of Aunt Viv."

"That's silly, Eva. He's a man." Best he explain Eva to the sheriff. "Eva has a big imagination. She don't know what she's talking about. You see, when I said what I said, I knew what I was talking for. I was just trying to scare him off. I never figured on him running and tattling to you."

"*Some* of your thinking makes good sense, but that don't subtract from the fact you lied. A good share of your thinking is mighty poor guessing. Still, it ain't uncommon to guess pretty wide and wild when you're concerned for the well-being of your loved ones. I guess you think a whole lot of this sister of yours and your G-Mama too. I won't hold your lying against you, but I still have to take you all into custody. Except Leatha. A good neighbor's a good neighbor."

"Custody? You taking us to jail?" yelled Adam. "I heard you was a hardhearted rascal. Well, that's mild naming!"

Eva said, "She is going to do it, Little Adam. She says G-Mama *has* to see a doctor and we cain't be left by ourselves. That the state *has* to take care of us. That means the orphan asylum again, I think, but she'll probably lock us all in jail first."

"Glory be!" roared Erica Wheeler. "This girl does have a wild imagination. Both of you do. You're twins all right. G-Mama, you know me better than that.

Tell these kids that I got to take you in against your will because their G-Mama is a stubborn old woman. Sometimes love gets in the way of good sense. A busted hip needs more than a home remedy. The doc lives three houses down from me. I'm taking you all to my house until G-Mama gets medical attention and we find someone to care for you properly. You're not going to rot in a jail cell."

G-Mama said, "Ericky, you cain't stop me from adopting these kids. If you'd kept your nose out, I'd been up and coming in town for them adoption papers in another three or four weeks at most."

Adam didn't know why G-Mama was tacking extra weeks on to her allotted healing time, but he didn't say anything.

Erica said, "G-Mama, love your soul, you cain't adopt these kids. The laws ain't made special for any one person. But we'll settle all that later. We just got to get you to the doctor and these kids . . ."

"All right. I'll marry Kirkwood. What makes the law think a single woman cain't raise kids? Widows do it all the time."

"Yeah. Widows do it all the time," said Adam. "Aunt Viv is raising her kids and she's a single woman like G-Mama."

"G-Mama has no use for Mr. Kirkwood," said Eva softly.

"Help me Hannah!" Erica twisted her tweed skirt all the way around and back again. "It ain't just because you're single. You're too *old*, G-Mama, and you're laid up. If you were in good health you could look after the kids, even if adopting would be out of the question. But you're not in good health."

"She will be," said Adam, "and all she'd have to do is live for eight more years and she'll do that easy, for she's from long-living stock. She says so!"

"Amen to that. I think she'll live to be a hundred, at least, but *I don't write the laws!* If I'd told those people at the asylum that you were seventy-five, they'd never let those kids come down here in the first place. Now stop acting like I'm against you."

It was a fact that Sheriff Erica Wheeler had been the one to get them back here. Though Adam had not let himself dwell on it, he'd seen too much concern on Leatha's face when she tended the hip, and he figured Erica Wheeler was more than right in saying G-Mama needed a doctor. G-Mama's injury was no secret anymore, so it was all right to let that worry come out in the open now. He moved over near where Leatha sat shelling peas. "G-Mama does need a doctor, don't she?" he whispered.

"That she do, Little Adam. She sure do."

"The sheriff's on our side. I guess we better go," announced Adam.

G-Mama groaned and Eva whispered to her, "We just don't know what poultice to try next, G-Mama. It'd be good to have you living right next to a doctor for a little while."

Well, that made everybody in favor of going for G-Mama's sake, but G-Mama. She wouldn't go quietly. "Ericky, all it takes to raise kids is a home and love and pep, and I got all three."

"What good is pep if you're down in bed? What you got is more confidence than you got sense, but I ain't holding that against you either. Leatha, you and Little Adam grab that end of her mattress, and Eva, you come help me with this end. Well move! Or do I have to draw my gun?"

They hauled G-Mama on her mattress out under the stars to Erica Wheeler's black pickup. G-Mama was yelling about her livestock.

Eva said, "We have to take Scrawny. He saved G-Mama's life."

"Bring your pup and go set up in the front seat. Leatha, you mind looking after G-Mama's livestock as long as Hank Furnet is looking after yours?"

"I'll be mighty glad to," said Leatha.

"Get your little fanny in here, Scrawny, and be quiet!" said Eva.

"What's that?" said G-Mama.

What had gotten into Eva? She was speaking sharply to Scrawny and acting like Miss Boss now that she was going to be sitting next to a sheriff. Eva continued in that same exacting tone. "G-Mama, stop complaining. You're getting that breath of fresh air and a change of scenery you been asking for."

Erica Wheeler was looking at Eva and smiling, and then she turned to Adam and said, "Well, if you ain't got anything you'd like to say, I guess we can leave you back here to care for G-Mama and get going. I'll drive slow."

"I got something I'd like to say," said Adam.

"Say it. We're all waiting," snapped G-Mama.

Sort of a relief had come to Adam to be leaving all the endless chores and garden and stuff that was new and hard for him. But on the other hand, he wanted the sheriff to know she wasn't just hauling off a ten-year-old boy that she could boss around.

He looked the sheriff right in the eye and said, "Scrawny ain't all Eva's dog. He's at least one-third mine. This afternoon he was barking like a crazy thing. I ran out to see what was the matter. It was broad daylight yet, mind you, and the wind was mild and the sun was low and hot. A great big old dark feathered buzzard was diving for a young pullet.

"Scrawny was raising such a racket that every one of that buzzard's dives got cut short, but he'd take off and come right back again. He meant business. I bet he'd already dived six or seven times and was likely to go seven or eight more and would have had that nice-sized pullet for sure."

"That's terrible," said G-Mama.

"Of course it was terrible. We needed all our chickens. Eggs are good as money at Kirkwood's store.

"Well, I knew that buzzard could peck out my eyes or at least leave a knot on my head, but I couldn't let G-Mama's pullet be caught up in them big ugly

137

wicked claws. I knew a rock would hardly slow down his flight. I knowed better than use my bare hands. I picked up a branch from the woodpile and started fighting that big old buzzard. The wind was rising a bit by now and the chickens were all cackling and of course Scrawny ain't stopped barking. I whooped a few whoops and I swatted and beat and flailed and that buzzard charged and recharged.

"We stirred up dust until there wasn't a clean spot on me, except my eyeballs. See for yourself. Anyway, no more'n five minutes and that was one scratched-up buzzard that took off for quieter country. I watched him sail out over that stretch of cleared ground and then sink into the darkness of the wood beyond. We still got our pullet."

G-Mama said, "Little Adam, hop in the truck bed and rest your mouth!"

Leatha said, "I'd better not forget to take in the eggs!"

Erica laid her hand on Adam's shoulder and said, "Thanks for that story. It was mighty entertaining and I'm proud to know you."

Well now, a woman who appreciates hearing a good true story couldn't be all bad. Yes, sir. It looked like that adoption would come off for sure. G-Mama could handle Hank Furnet if he was the one to be sheriff, and Adam felt he himself might just be able to handle Erica Wheeler. She sure seemed to like a boy who could beat off a big mean buzzard.

eleven

Erica Wheeler had a big house sitting on a corner lot. One corner of the house was rounded, including the big window that allowed viewing down both streets. This window was full of houseplants which Erica rearranged to make room for G-Mama's bed. It really wasn't a bad place at all, but G-Mama refused to be happy that first day. "A prison is a prison no matter what color you paint the walls."

But even G-Mama could see after the first day that being there wasn't all bad. Maybe Erica was a little bit of a bully when it came to eating and chores and stuff. She was forever looking at the gold watch that she wore on a chain around her neck. She timed you for washing up and for eating.

She also forced you to eat your bacon and to do the dishes along with Eva. G-Mama had to be forced to eat at doctor's orders. She gagged on every mouthful. But things really weren't that bad.

Both Adam and Eva had feather ticks to sleep on, and Erica had cleaned out a big curved top trunk to hold their clothes. With all of them there, the house still wasn't overcrowded to speak of, so it did make a body wonder how one person had managed to use up all this space before.

Adam told Eva, "G-Mama'll settle in. She'll take to this place sooner or later; she'd be nuts not to."

G-Mama heard him. Sometimes she was too old to hear good and other times she could hear when you were way on the other side of the big living room. She shouted, "I'll take to nothing in this life unless I've a mind to. Ericky could keep me here a hundred years and I'd not settle in unless I had a mind to."

Adam had had enough. "Look here, G-Mama, you ain't really trying. Me and Eva ain't complaining. We've gone along with everything because we don't want to be sent back to the orphan asylum where things are really bad. I tell you, G-Mama, sorry as you think things are here at Erica's, things could be worse."

"I doubt it. That was the stringiest oatmeal I ever ate in my life. She ought to know enough to cook it in water instead of milk, and it wouldn't string from your spoon like that."

Adam snapped, "I made that oatmeal! Maybe I ain't a hundred percenter on cooking but I did it.

I didn't go bellyaching for my thank-you neither."

Eva came over to join in the talk. "Little Adam, I can see where your oatmeal would make anyone go off their food. I'd have said something myself if there wasn't someone with a watch and a gun sitting at the same table with me. Lots of sick people go off their food and get skinny. Uncle Burl did once. Then Aunt Viv fried him up some crusty cornbread and smeared mustard on it, and his appetite came back."

G-Mama lay there with the sun streaking in across her bed, thinking. Then she crooned, "Eva, could I get you to make me a batch of fried cornbread?"

Eva did it and G-Mama ate every morsel, said it tasted good and laid good on her stomach too. Then she took on new life and started giving orders. "Ericky may be firm and prompt, but we can still give her a hand. Little Adam, get the pail. Eva, find the clean rags. We're going to wash windows."

What did she mean *we*? It was him and Eva who did the work. After she had worked them half to death, G-Mama allowed it was time again to take her medicine, as long as she was being forced by the law to do it.

Eva had lain down in front of the big curved window, sunning. She sighed. "And I got to bathe you. I'm tired, G-Mama."

G-Mama said, "Little Adam, bring me a wash pan and soap. I can bathe myself. And both of you can step outside. I ain't sick anymore, and I got a right to

141

a little modesty. That alcohol-soaked rag I put around my neck last night must be helping."

It was likely that it was all that stuff the doctor gave her that was helping, but there was no point in arguing. Adam gladly went outside and played statue for a while with Eva. Then he let Eva convince him and Scrawny to play hide-and-go-seek with her. That went along all right until Eva let him count to a hundred and yell "Ready!" and then was impossible to find. She didn't come when he yelled, "Allie, Allie, outs in free." He hunted for her more and then found her in by G-Mama's big bed fast asleep. So was G-Mama.

Adam picked up the wash pan from the bedside table and threw the sudsy water outside. Sure didn't look like Eva was having nightmares, and it sure did look like G-Mama was mending fast. A crazy thought flitted right through his mind and out again. Sheriffs ain't mothers.

Sheriff Erica Wheeler came home that evening and commented, "I never knowed what a difference shining windows could make. It does sort of change things around this house, or is it something more than that?"

G-Mama said, "If Adam would get me some cane and split it, I'd fix that chair bottom for you, Ericky. My hands has started itching to do some work."

So for the next few days, he did things like that for G-Mama when she asked, or if she didn't ask, he just loafed around town watching the day begin and finish without worrying about a thing. One evening after a quiet day, when supper was over, when the street-lights had come on and everyone was settling down for the night, Adam asked Erica Wheeler a favor. "You know how to play that harmonica?"

"Oh, fair to middling," she said. "I ain't too musical, but my pa played pretty good and he taught me. I used to walk his rounds with him and it give me something to do. Wasn't any use me staying home, my ma was dead. Died when I was five and a half."

Eva said, "I play guitar right well. I take after my daddy. You ever go out near G-Mama's place, I'd like you to bring her guitar back here. I miss it."

"Check on Leatha," said G-Mama, "and see if she's slopping the hogs and keeping the cow milked. She's probably got milk going to waste. Tell her to give the hogs the whey, but bring in the top cream. I think if someone props me up in the right way, I could churn some butter."

Adam went on with his request. "I was wondering if you ever let anybody touch your harmonica?"

Erica Wheeler must not have heard him, for she answered G-Mama, "I'll take a run out tomorrow. First I'll check with the doctor. If he says we can prop you up so your feet can dangle to the side of the bed, I'll bring back some cream. By the way, Doc says you don't have to lather up every time you bathe, three—four times a day. It's to control your temperature, not to get off dirt. You'll get all the natural oils out of your skin."

"Then bring me that can of goose grease on the left-hand top shelf of the kitchen cabinet. Whoever heard of washing without soap? And you bring me that cream. We been eating you out of house and home, and it's time we're helping out."

Erica said, "If Eva will make up a list, I'll get whatever you want . . . that is, if you'd come along and help me collect it, Little Adam."

"I sure will. You think we ought to leave Scrawny here or take him along?"

"Better leave Scrawny home. You might want to bring along the harmonica. It's a pretty long ride. Give you something to do."

Well, that sure gave him something to sleep on. A harmonica had never touched his lips. Boy, he was coming closer and closer to really liking it at Erica Wheeler's house.

The next day, the beginning of the ride with Erica was the beginning of his lessons on the harmonica. Erica Wheeler said there wasn't much to it excepting blowing out and sucking in, and those two talents was what most good storytellers was born with. She laughed hearty and things went pleasant.

After he'd sucked in and blowed out about a million times, he chose to shake the spit out and give it a rest. He put it in his shirt pocket and asked, "Erica Wheeler, why ain't you married? Is it against the law

144

for sheriffs to marry?" She didn't answer right off and he felt foolish for meddling. "I guess I ought not to stick my nose in other people's business."

"If you was a grown-up, I guess I'd agree with you on that point. But since you're not, I'd say it's just innocence and will answer. No reason not to tell you, I reckon. I loved a man once. Maybe I still do. You know him. The man you told that big lie to, Hank Furnet. Well, he had one set of ideas and I had another. I guess according to his law, sheriffs cain't marry. Or more accurate, you cain't marry if you want to stay being sheriff." It seemed hard for her to go on.

"And you wanted to stay being sheriff."

"I knew the work inside and out. I like being sheriff. Besides, I promised my daddy to carry on for him. Maybe I was too set in my ways. Sometimes I've regretted it." She was talking soft and longingly. He knew she had slipped and let herself talk like this and that he must never repeat a thing he heard to a living soul. Not even if it'd make good listening.

"Your secret is good with me," he told her.

She come alert and then slapped him on the back and laughed. "I believe it is. You're all right, Little Adam. Just fine."

He laughed too and and asked, "Is it true that you chased the hoochie-coochie dancers out of the carnival at Bernie?"

She roared with laughter this time but didn't an-

145

swer, just rushed her truck to a hard fast stop in front of G-Mama's cabin. They got all the stuff on the list and more besides. Adam gathered stuff from the garden. Leatha apologized for not so much top cream. She hadn't wanted it to go to waste and had shared some with Mr. Jones, Mr. Silts' overseer.

"It's all right," said Adam. "G-Mama will be right happy with all your caring and help."

And indeed, when they got back home, G-Mama was pleased with about everything. She got herself propped up just right and pushed the dasher up and down in her old wooden churn until the top cream turned into golden butter. She salted it and patted it and molded it. Eva had to lay an oilcloth on her bed to save the sheets, but everybody was happy to see G-Mama acting fit again.

Erica ordered Adam and Eva to go out and play under the streetlights and get to know some of the neighbor kids. Adam didn't know about that, but he went. He took Scrawny and Erica's harmonica along. He leaned up against the light post and played "Twinkle, Twinkle, Little Star."

Scrawny went yipping over to where three girls were singing. Two of them were clapping away on each other's hands, and the other girl was *thump, thump*ing with her jump rope as she jumped and sang along with them. They stopped to talk to Scrawny and then came over to Eva and Adam. The one who'd been jumping the rope said, "Did the sheriff haul you in?"

"Nobody hauled me in!"

"I heard Erica Wheeler did, and she's sheriff and she's a woman too. Ha, ha, ha!"

Adam shoved his harmonica back into his shirt pocket and grabbed one of the girls' red pigtails in his hand. "What's her being a woman got to do with it?" he demanded.

He couldn't exactly say what happened next, but pretty soon he was fighting off four girls; one of them was his sister Eva. It was a swell fight, Scrawny growling deep in his throat, all seemed topsy-turvy. It never did come to an end, for Erica Wheeler come out and broke in on it.

Adam grabbed Scrawny and dashed toward the house. "I hope you was on my side, Scrawny. Were you?" Scrawny curled into a little ball and nuzzled up close. That was when Adam discovered the harmonica was missing from his pocket and had to go back and pick it up off the ground. He knocked the dirt out, for the holes had gotten all plugged. He was forced to go in and wash it out and blow it dry so it wouldn't rust.

Erica never mentioned the dropped harmonica even once, though he was sure she saw him cleaning it. She didn't mention it even when she was reporting the goings on to G-Mama. "Wow, of all the fights I've broken up, this one was the worse."

Adam couldn't resist helping her tell the facts. "Yep, it was a bad one, almost as bad as the fight I had with that big buzzard, but not quite. Still this one had its share of scratching and clawing and biting and squealing. Girl fighting and buzzard fighting have a lot in common."

Erica laughed. "You got yourself another story to tell, Little Adam? Believe him, G-Mama, them girls was laying into him and he was giving it all he had. G-Mama, how's a woman your age going to handle a couple kids like these?"

"They ain't always rowdy," G-Mama said. Thank goodness G-Mama held her tongue. Maybe she was catching on that it was smartest not to sass Erica so much.

Adam had the harmonica blown quite dry again and was getting "Twinkle, Twinkle, Little Star" to come out good as ever.

Erica asked him, "How'd you like to bring that harmonica along and go the rounds with me tomorrow?"

Well, he liked that idea real fine, and when he and Eva were nestled down into their featherbeds, he whispered that fact to her. "And you know something else, Eva? I think I like living here and I think I like Erica's beau too. She just may marry him someday."

That wasn't really telling Erica's secret. He didn't tell Eva any more details of what Erica had told him. He felt right good inside and was curled up sound asleep before he knew it.

He was startled awake soon enough by Eva having another nightmare. She said that she dreamed that

Mr. Furnet was a huge giant with a mustache ten feet long. He had come and wrapped that mustache around Erica Wheeler and had carted her away.

"That's silly, Eva. No man can wrap a mustache around a sheriff. Git back to sleep. Mr. Furnet is a nice man."

"I don't like him. He reminds me of Aunt Viv."

Erica called in to see if everything was all right and Adam assured her it was. And he guessed it really was, for Eva did settle down and go back to sleep and never had no more nightmares the rest of the night.

The next day Adam, with his harmonica, walked around town with Sheriff Erica Wheeler. She knew just about everybody and stopped here and there to chat. Adam worked away on his harmonica until he had it making a sound just like a real freight train by the end of the day. A sound that really got Scrawny a-going.

Right when Erica said they'd better go home and see about supper, a man came running up. "Ericky, the phone operator says you're to get out to Kirkwood's general store in the country. He says he's got a prowler in his storage room!"

Erica ran for her truck, and Adam and Scrawny ran right with her and jumped in alongside her. They never slowed down again until they were in front of Mr. Kirkwood's store. He was out front waiting for them. He said, "He caught me unprepared. I only keep this place heavy padlocked at night. I thought I

149

heard a doorknob turn, but I listened for the screech of hinges and heard nothing. So I opened the door to the back room and I see these beady eyes looking at me like two snakes looking at a bird."

Erica asked, "Is he still there? Did you say anything to him before you called for me?"

"He's still in there, all right. Oh, I could have taken a swing at him with my cane, but I was afraid I'd knock his head off if I swung at 'im in the dark like that. My storage room's got no windows."

"Well, I'm against swinging in the dark myself. I'll just drive my truck up to the back door and turn on the headlights so we can see what's going on in there. Adam, I'll let you set here in the truck if you promise to get Scrawny and yourself down under the dashboard if there's call for shooting."

Erica got the truck around in proper position and turned on the light. She got out, drew her gun and called, "Come out, whoever's in there."

"You come in here!" came back the answer.

"All right. I'm coming in and I got my gun drawn."

"Forget I said anything," the voice called back. Erica, holding her gun in hand, walked over and opened the back door. There stood a man with a flat bald head, blinded by the light, and holding a potato sack full of stuff. Erica put her gun back in its holster, took the bag and said, "This your stuff, Kirkwood? Howdy, Gus."

Mr. Kirkwood looked inside and said, "That's

mine. He's punched a hole in the top of this peanut butter bucket and has et quite a glob of it. I was trying to pry the lid off that myself this morning." With that, Mr. Kirkwood kicked a few car tools aside to join others in a heap by the building. "Gus, what makes you sneaking? You sharecropping for Silts. He could go you for some grocery credit."

The bald-headed man didn't say anything.

Erica said, "You already asked Silts and he said no, right Gus?"

The man nodded.

"Well, you get on home. I'll come out to settle with you on this later." Gus took off running.

"Don't go easy on him, Ericky. He owes me for that peanut butter he et."

"Kirkwood, I'm obliged to handle things the way I see best; unless the judge tells me different, that's what I'll do. Adam, it's about time me and you went home for supper. Seeing all that peanut butter is making me hungry."

When they got back inside the truck, Adam asked, "You ever kill a bad guy?"

"Not if there is any earthly way for me to keep from it. We're all human beings. One cain't lose sight of that. Gus Marlo was hungry."

"Mr. Kirkwood says you got to do something to him for his eating that peanut butter."

"Don't mention peanut butter again when I'm starved."

151

Adam let it ride for a while and then told Erica, "You know what I was going to do if that man was still hiding when you opened the door? I was going to turn Scrawny loose and say, 'Sic 'im, boy. Roust out the robber, Scrawny!' and I bet he would have too."

"Is that a fact?" said Erica Wheeler, and she drove on home.

After they'd had a good supper of wilted lettuce, fried potatoes, and hot biscuits and butter, Erica said, "G-Mama, Gus Marlo's family is hard put for food. If it's all right with you, I'd like to take him the rest of the bread and the butter and maybe we can bag up a few potatoes too."

Adam spoke up real fast. "Sure you can, and you can tell him to go get some of the turnips and stuff from G-Mama's garden too."

Erica looked at G-Mama and smiled. "That suggestion set right with you, G-Mama?"

Again Adam spoke fast. "Sure, G-Mama is proud to share."

As it turned out, Adam was exactly right as he knew he would be. G-Mama was proud to share as long as Gus Marlo asked Leatha first. Adam was proud to go along with Erica to deliver that message to Gus Marlo. Proud as could be to rumble along in Erica's truck over wooden bridges and gravel road to Gus Marlo's place. But he was puzzled about the way Erica handled the law.

"Why ain't you arresting him and making him pay

for the peanut butter?" Adam asked after they left Gus Marlo's place.

"Ain't no sense in it. Hunger muddles and confuses a man's mind. He'll straighten up when his family ain't starving. I figure it helps G-Mama to be helping someone too. Maybe she won't rankle so easy being cooped up like she is."

"Nope, I don't reckon she'll rankle so easy anymore That's a fact," said Adam.

They drove a little further on and Erica braked the truck to a stop alongside of one of the wooden bridges. "I might as well check out that Wilson kid's tale as long as we're out in these parts. He claims he was playing down here by the bridge a couple of weeks ago and saw a hand of a skeleton sticking up out of the brush. He felt sure it was a hand, for he says he saw a ring on a finger."

Adam really didn't want to see a skeleton. But neither did he not want to see it. He followed Erica Wheeler to a pile of brush caught in the water's edge at the foot of the bridge. She started pulling branches out, so he lit right in and helped. There wasn't any skeleton.

"You think it got washed away?"

"Who knows? Things like that should be reported at once. The boy told me today that he's spoken of it to his folks at the time he'd seen it. They were all afraid of being blamed if they told me, I guess, so nothing was said until the boy came in town today and told me himself. Lots of things could happen in two weeks. And maybe there was nothing here to begin with. Maybe what he saw was just a nice bony twig with a bit of tinfoil from a gum wrapper caught on it, and he mistook it for a ring. Cain't always trust your mind to interpret accurately what the eyes see."

"You know what I'd have done if I was his folks and was afraid of getting blamed?"

"No, Little Adam, I don't."

"Well, I would have wrote you an anonymous letter and told you right off. Or maybe I'd have wrapped a handkerchief over the mouthpiece of the phone and called you in a strange voice."

"Is that a fact?" said Erica, taking off her shoes and wading out in the water to give everything a good once-over. "Water's deep. Mud is settled and packed to a smooth floor."

Adam continued to help her solve her problem. "You know, maybe his folks was here. Maybe they was trying to save that person and had to let go or drown. You know, a drowning person is ten times stronger in their panic. If you try to help too much, both of you will drown. And if that person had've drowned and they felt like they was the cause, then they'd not likely report it, now would they?"

"Adam, I think you're going to be right good when it comes to law."

Adam reckoned she was right. He reckoned she was right about a lot of things. He felt now was as

154

good a time as any to discuss something with her. He planned to ask her what could be done about Eva getting adopted if G-Mama couldn't do it, but that wasn't the question that came out. "G-Mama ever going to be up and about?" he asked.

Now why did he ask that? He hadn't known that he'd even allowed such a thought. Erica Wheeler just stood there looking at him, letting the water lap about her feet as she said ever so softly, "The doctor don't expect she will. She's old and it's her hip."

"I didn't ruin it when I jerked it, did I?"

"No, Doc said that part was fine. But bones don't knit the same in older bodies."

"What are we going to do? Eva needs adopting bad!"

"An what about you, Little Adam Braggs? What do you need?"

"I don't need nothing. Nothing at all!"

"Yes, you do. And if I wasn't single, I'd adopt you both." Then Erica got silent, almost like she was embarrassed or . . . scared. It was hard to figure a woman sheriff out.

Adam sensed his thoughts going soft. "I'll catch you some crawdads. See all them chimneys of mud? I bet I can get us a big mess of crawdad tails."

"That sounds hunky-dory to me. Go get 'em, rascal," Erica answered.

He got them and got them plenty. Dressed out, he had a good half quart of crawdad tails to show

155

G-Mama when they got back home. G-Mama told Eva how to spice them and cook them. Then they all sat around awfully happy there at Erica Wheeler's eating crawdad tails, picking the guitar, playing the harmonica and singing. Boy, he'd give anything to keep it this way. Now he hadn't asked Erica Wheeler to say what she said down by that bridge. She had just out and said it of her own accord.

Mr. Kirkwood had said he figured that Hank Furnet had come back to marry Erica. She still pined for the man. Only Adam knew that fact. With all sides being so willing, even though far apart, it shouldn't take any skill at all to get Erica Wheeler married and him and Eva adopted. He'd wait until Saturday. Everybody comes into town on Saturdays. He'd need a couple of days anyway to think up what to say to a perfect stranger. It wouldn't be proper to come right out plain and ask the man if he'd please marry Erica Wheeler.

twelve

It was scary. He had busted his brains thinking and it hadn't done any good. Now he must go and do it, scary or not. A certain amount of waiting and putting off can be tolerated in oneself but past that, there has to be action created somehow. Erica's beau, Hank Furnet, had not showed up on Saturday. Adam waited. But he didn't show up the following Saturday either. Now it was Monday, and somehow Adam had to be sure that Hank Furnet would be in town by the upcoming Saturday. He got a penny postcard from G-Mama and wrote on it:

Dear Mr. Furnet: There's been some cars speeding through Bernie. Better come in town Saturday and check on it, since you are a high-way patrol.

A citizen

G-Mama thought he got the card to write to Aunt Dory, and he let her go on believing that; he didn't need no sass to keep him from doing what had to be done. It took courage to do it in the first place. No sooner had he mailed the card than he was sure it was a dumb idea and would never work. Maybe Hank Furnet had gone back to Illinois already; maybe that's why he hadn't shown up. Maybe getting him to marry Erica was a dumb idea too. Maybe all this waiting was a warning to him. Well, he couldn't call back a card sent in the mail. Mail always gets delivered. It was a long stretch between Monday and Saturday but he had no choice now but to wait it out.

He escaped the folds of his feather tick by five o'clock Saturday morning and reported only to G-Mama as he left. "Tell everyone, I'm out chasing around town with Scrawny. Bye." He didn't wait to hear any remarks G-Mama might have.

He waited around for maybe four or four-and-a half hours when someone yelled, "Here comes Silts' Model-T." Everyone around town knew of Silts' Model-T, how he kept it shining and as new-looking as the day it was purchased. So when the car pulled to a stop, some men crowded around and Adam sidled over to join the crowd himself. Let people think it was to see the car if they wished, but it was really because Hank Furnet was sitting in that car along with Mr. Silts.

"Looks plum new," said one old man.

"Good as new," announced Mr. Silts, tipping his hat and swinging his cane as he got out. "I bought this car new back when me and the missus was first married. Took every cent we could scrap up past the farm and personal needs. Hard times was at their worst. The man who bought it never drove it but once. Then he found out he couldn't meet the payments and pay for the gas to feed it, too. So he set it up on blocks and almost a year later I took it off his hands and kept up the payments. Its a sporty car and worth taking care of."

Adam let the men admire Mr. Silts' car but he himself was admiring Hank Furnet. He was as fine a looking man as the Model-T was a fine-looking car. He'd make a right nice father for Eva. Why, Mr. Furnet's shoulders were almost as big as Mr. Jones's.

Mr. Silts must have caught Adam eyeing Hank Furnet, for he right away started introducing Hank Furnet to the men, calling each by name. When he got to Adam, Mr. Silts said, "I don't know the boy's name myself."

Mr. Furnet said, "I met the boy before. He come over to Kirkwood's store when I was there. Your G-Mama recovering from her contagious disease?"

Gosh dang, he'd forgotten about that lie he'd told Mr. Furnet. What's worse than lying is lying to a highway patrol. Maybe he wouldn't be so forgiving as Sheriff Erica Wheeler. Until he found out for sure, he felt it best to change the subject—fast. "G-Mama's fine. We're over visiting for a spell with the sheriff. Now there's a woman that any man would be lucky to have. A fine woman. Finer than this car. Finer than . . ." Adam had run out of words.

Mr. Furnet cocked his head to one side and his eyes laughed from beneath those dark eyebrows. He stroked his red mustache and said, "Finer than any woman in these parts. I was of the same opinion once myself."

Mr. Silts had stood listening. "No reason why you still cain't be. You know Ericky always has carried around that little gold watch you gave her. Not everybody knows that, but she has it on a chain around her neck, and that's a fact."

Adam hadn't planned on anyone's help but was thankful for it. Well, Mr. Silts' words sure had lit up the features of Hank Furnet.

"Is that right?" said Hank Furnet.

"Absolutely right!" said Adam. "And there's another fact you might be interested in. We're going on a picnic this afternoon down by the schoolhouse near the bridge. I'd just be pleased as could be to have you join us."

"Name the time."

"Four o'clock," called Adam, and he started right away to race home so as to let everyone know they were going on a picnic. He wasn't so fast though, as to not hear Mr. Furnet's last comment. "I'll be there, if I ain't held up clocking speeders." Geewhizamighty, there was no way that Mr. Furnet could

160

have known who wrote him that card. But then one never knows about the law—they got ways. Still, Mr. Furnet looked pleased, and that was the thing to ponder. Why, with Hank Furnet being a cop and Erica being a sheriff, when they got married and adopted him, he'd then become a son-of-the-law. It sounded great.

Eva never caught on to his excitement at all, nor his clever joke. She said, "I don't like that man. Let him talk and you'll see. Erica don't like him either."

"She does too. Eva, you don't help me and you don't help yourself talking like that. I think Erica will marry him."

G-Mama said, "I don't see why you're so dead set on matchmaking, but I guess it's just as well. I'm mending fast and this house is going to seem empty to Ericky when we all leave." Then G-Mama directed her talk to Eva. "Eva, use them leftover mashed potatoes, add a little garlic and hot pepper, and make sandwiches. What's Ericky say about this picnic?"

Adam said, "Oh, she's going to like the idea. I'm going to go tell her right now. Just wanted something going here first." He ran about the dusty streets of Bernie until he found Erica, and right away she knew he needed help in saying something, for she asked, "Got a locked jaw, have you?"

"Maybe if you'd draw your gun and force me, it'd come easier," Adam said, pleased at his own cleverness again.

Erica became stern, if not downright mad. "Never

161

joke about this gun, Little Adam. I never risk an accident with such horsing around. A bullet takes its path whether it's shot accidental or on purpose. Now say what you come to say!"

That just about took the wind of happiness right out of him, but he spluttered out what he'd rehearsed. "I asked Mr. Furnet to come to a picnic with us at four o'clock down by the schoolhouse near the bridge."

It sounded awfully ridiculous and pushy and just plain silly once it was said out loud to her. Dangit, whangit, why had he ever let himself get carried away with such wild notions in the first place?

"I take it as a compliment that you want to help me, Little Adam. Maybe I need help. I wasn't likely to go asking Hank myself. Folks has been saying he's back in town on account of me. I've talked a bit to him once, but nothing was said, really. Maybe we need you, Little Adam."

"He wanted to see you. I know he did." That's what that twinkle in Mr. Furnet's eye meant, so it was all right to say that.

"I expect you're right. Mr. Silts has told me over the years that Hank has asked of me. But then he was married . . . had a family. Okay, let's go tell G-Mama and Eva."

Adam didn't care to comment on that. He just followed her on home. It hadn't occurred to him not to tell G-Mama first. It is hard when you have to answer to two women in the household.

G-Mama's greeting was, "Ericky, get your hair fixed. Use the curling iron on Eva too, and don't frizz it. Her hair's fine as goose down. So you're going along with Adam's matchmaking, are you? I always heard Hank Furnet was no good behind a plow, and couldn't hold up his end of the load on some other things, but maybe he'll be better as a cop. Kirkwood seems to think so. Go on now, and don't worry about me. I'm well. I'll set right here and be waiting when you return. Just leave me a sandwich."

Erica pulled the watch up from where it dangled under her shirt. She checked the time. Then she heated the curling iron in the lamp chimney and did Eva's hair so it bent into an outward curl just where it touched her shoulders. Erica's own hair was short, so she did a couple fast clamps with the curling iron to set some waves in it. It frizzed a little in one spot, but she spit on it and laid it flat with her fingers.

Adam pretended he was going to curl Scrawny's fur while Erica went to change her clothes.

Eva's hair looked right nice, but her face was sad. "I don't want to go to a picnic if that Hank Furnet man is there."

Erica came back in wearing a dress flimsy as a curtain. She got her gun and hung it back on her hip. It looked twice as big for some reason, hanging there on that dress. But she had to be sheriff round the clock, he guessed. Or was Erica still making it clear that she wasn't quitting sheriffing?

Erica smiled and touched Eva's shoulder, and

163

G-Mama rattled right along with her talking. "You're a right nice-looking woman, Ericky, and I'm thinking Hank Furnet ought to have done right, been less contrary years ago. I hear he's got a mustache now. I'd make him shave that off before I'd marry him if I was you. Did I ever tell you about the time I singed . . .?"

"You did," said Erica. "I don't begrudge a man his mustache, and anyway, I ain't getting married today. Give me a couple of days, okay?"

G-Mama went right on talking. "I remember when Hank was young and got his right eye hurt. That might be what's got Eva reading something into him that ain't so. From then on he always had to cock his head just a bit to see people right. Never served as no handicap. Gave him kind of a cute look when he was little, and he made the most of it. Turn that wick down on that lamp; the chimney's getting all smoked up."

Erica blew out the lamp. "There, we're done anyway. Little Adam, you better put in a new wick; that one's too short already. Eva, what else do we need in the food bucket?"

Adam set the lamp on the floor and started to change the wick, but Scrawny grabbed it and started dragging it across the floor. It was like the whole household was nervous. It was a great relief when they got everything in the bucket, got messages left around town where to find Erica, in case, and finally got to the picnic spot.

164

Hank Furnet was standing by the edge of a little grove of oak trees, waiting. He had a case of Pepsi cooling down in the water; some of the labels already had soaked loose. Mr. Furnet's husky "Howdy Ericky" was a welcome sound. He joined Erica Wheeler, and the two of them walked aside. Later they walked over to check on the soda pop with Adam. Erica's dress swept easily with the wind, and her gun reflected sunlight with every stride. She was a right pretty woman, for a fact.

Mr. Furnet said, "There ain't much fire in them bottles, but I figgered it'd make you remember the time in Kansas City." He never explained to Adam and Eva what that meant, and Adam thought it best not to ask. Anyway, the Pepsi was cool and good, and they could have all they wanted of it.

Adam had to make Eva stop gulping so he could catch all the stuff Mr. Furnet was telling Erica. He told about the time he got fired from a job once, just because he showed up late that one time; and about the time, since he was made highway patrol, that he stopped some men who'd just bought themselves a bunch of counterfeit nickels. "I knowed they was counterfeit the minute I see the shine on 'em. Full of lead and had too much glass in 'em. I hauled them jackals right over to the Feds. I hear all three of them got sent to the pen, but one got religion while there and got set free."

It looked as if this kind of talk could go on forever if Adam didn't jump in there and give Erica some help. He put his Pepsi aside, went over, and sat facing Hank Furnet. "You know, my Uncle Windy knew this man who married a woman just three weeks and three days after he met her. Three weeks and two days after they met, the man asked her to marry him, and right away she said yes." Adam paused for effect.

Mr. Furnet said, "Well, I guess that broke him of that asking habit, didn't it?"

Adam went ahead and laughed along with Mr. Furnet, even though that was not what he'd expected to be said. He continued. "That couple was engaged for exactly fifteen hours; then they got married and right after that went to the Blinking Owl, bought two soda pops, and went home."

"That's an entertaining story, Little Adam, and we thank you," said Erica with an awful lot of politeness in her voice.

"The man was some kind of fool," said Mr. Furnet. "No man should marry with his head in a poke. One of my cousins married a woman on the spur of the moment like that and come to find out she had a bone problem, and she ended up crippled and there he was . . . stuck. I know what it is to be around a crippled girl. I went to school with one. Her mother was an odd one. Never would let her sit down because it would mess up her dress. She looked better standing up. Course she had to sit down at school."

Eva put down her soda pop and said, "Mr. Furnet, you ain't got enough brains to blow up a paper bag!"

166

Erica was standing up now, adjusting her gun and smoothing her dress, although it wasn't a bit winkled. Adam whispered, "What's got into Eva?"

Eva said, quite loudly. "That man don't know what it's like being around a crippled girl, even if he was in the same school with one. My friend Esther is nice to be around. She's my best friend!" Eva's voice was getting mean.

Erica said quickly, "Hank, these children have lost their uncles, who were like fathers to them, and . . ."

"Yeah, I heard that the Braggs boys was drunker than lords. Heard too that Windy's truck wasn't worth the name after it got hit. Must have really been speeding. Boy, that was awful. No, I guess they never knew what hit them. Really bad."

Adam's head was clear and sober, and he knew what had hit him. He and Eva were going to have to stay orphans forever if it depended on Erica marrying this man. He'd never allow it! Uncle Windy always told him to harbor no evil in his soul, but he couldn't help it. The worst part, even worse than the words, was that Hank Furnet had a twinkle in his eye all the while he was talking!

Silence came and stayed. No one moved, or spoke.

The cows were moaning and crowding near the fence. Overhead the sun had been blotted out until the other side of tomorrow. A cloud of gnats peppered their faces. Mr. Furnet was the first to announce, "A storm's a-brewing. Take cover!" He headed towards the boy's outhouse by the school. Erica and Eva headed for the truck. Adam went to grab Scrawny and then chose not to go to the truck just yet. He ran after Hank Furnet. The rain broke before he made it to the outhouse door. He didn't care. He simply turned the outside latch, locking Hank Furnet into the toilet. Then, laughing in the rain, he and Scrawny ran back to join Erica and Eva in the truck. Now what would they tell G-Mama?

G-Mama greeted them with, "You get rained out? Where's Hank Furnet?"

Erica spoke first. "We had a fine picnic. I wouldn't have missed it for all the timber in the North woods. Either I was blind when I was younger, or Mr. Hank Furnet has done a lot of changing in the last eighteen years. As to where he is right now, I don't care."

G-Mama wanted a few more details, so Adam, with Eva's help, supplied them for her.

"Still in the outhouse, you say? Serves him right. Someone ought to shoot him and put him out of his misery. I've heard it said, Ericky, that any man is better than no man, but I've always took issue on that statement. Glad to see that you do too, girl."

"You still keeping that watch?" Adam asked Erica.

She pulled it out from under her dress collar and looked at it for a long moment. "That was a lot of years I spent of needless yearning for a man I don't care for now." She dropped the watch back on its chain. "Why shouldn't I keep it? Still keeps good time." She stood there still for another minute and then said, "The show's running a special rate tonight . . . five cents. You two want to see a movie?"

Eva was so happy, she was fairly dancing. Adam wanted to see the movie too, but it hurt to see Eva so happy here. It wasn't going to last. There was no way she was going to get adopted by Erica Wheeler now . . . or by anybody.

thirteen

Adam was still blaming himself for not seeing beyond
Hank Furnet's mustache. But G-Mama comforted
him by saying, "Freshness of the weather is a right
time for renewal. Look to the rain. We all need a
time of renewal in our thoughts and lives."

So Adam had already gotten himself feeling better
when Mr. Kirkwood dropped in with money for the
eggs Leatha had taken him.

Mr. Kirkwood brought other news too. "Ericky,
I'm afraid you hurt Hank Furnet's feelings. Word's
spread around pretty fast that he got low treatment
from you. He told me he's going to be here only a
couple more days until Judge Nagle comes and can
settle the title on that place of his. Then he'll go back
and take up his highway patrol job in Illinois."

"Oh? He sell his place?" asked Erica, just as if she

was more interested in a bit of news than she was in Mr. Furnet. At least she could have asked how he got out of the outhouse.

"Yep, he sold it. Fact, he sold it to the likeliest of persons—Leatha. She and that Mr. Jones is getting hitched. Black people got more sense than white. Ericky, you ain't no spring chicken no more. You ought to be marrying and settling down. It's embarrassing to a grown man to have to scream his head off while standing in a locked outhouse. Double so, if he has to stay there all night until a couple of old women, on their way to church, finds him. I don't blame him one bit for selling out and moving back to Illinois. You missed a good chance, Ericky." Mr. Kirkwood looked directly at G-Mama as he said that last statement.

Let G-Mama quarrel back at him if she liked, Adam wouldn't be listening. He wouldn't even allow himself the time to fully enjoy the overnight aggravation he'd caused Mr. Furnet, as rightfully as he deserved it. There was new joy to take hold on. Mr. Kirkwood had let out a piece of wonderful news: Judge Nagle was due in town in a couple of days.

All the while Adam had been swinging on the potato sack swing, he'd been thinking. All the while he'd been honing the kitchen knives until he'd worn out a whetstone, he'd been thinking. All the while he'd sat playing "Red River Valley" on the harmonica, he'd been thinking. And his thinking had

171

come to this: He'd have to talk some sense into the judge.

G-Mama's sass had finally gotten Mr. Kirkwood to the point that he said he'd better get going. Adam felt grateful to him for the news about the judge and wanted to let him leave with something more than sass. "Thanks for dropping off the money for the eggs. Say thanks to Leatha for collecting them. Well, thanks to you, Mr. Kirkwood, for everything."

Both G-Mama and Erica gave him approving looks for such politeness, and Adam settled comfortably, rehearsing to himself what he was going to say to the judge. He rehearsed for the rest of that day and all the next day, and all that rehearsing paid off. He was able to let the words come out fast and natural the minute he saw Judge Nagle.

"Judge, is it actually against the law for a single woman to adopt kids? Why would it be when a widow woman does it all the time? Aunt Viv is finishing raising her kids and Uncle Burl is dead. She ain't the best mother in the world neither, but no law tried to stop her."

"Boy, you preaching or asking a question?"

"Asking a question. Can a single woman adopt two kids?"

"It could be done, I reckon, if there was some rare exception to the rule. But, you see, the laws are made to protect kids, and a woman without steady work might not be able to give a child the care."

172

"What if she had steady work?"

"Then she'd not likely be considered right either. Kids need someone home to care for them properly. I know some widows have it bad and have to work, but that come about by an act of God, not of the courts. Why all the concern; you got a case in mind?"

"I could have. Thanks a lot!" Adam ran through the streets of Bernie shouting, "Sheriff! Sheriff!" Scrawny had found him now and was barking to help draw attention, and sure enough, in no time he got directed to Erica.

"Adam, what's the matter? Hold on here, what's wrong?"

"Come home quick. I cain't talk until we get there." He knew he was scaring Erica, but she'd be very happy later. They both burst in through the front door, and Adam started to yell for G-Mama and Eva, but . . .

"G-Mama! G-Mama! You all right, G-Mama?"

There was Eva sitting by G-Mama where she lay on the floor. Eva sobbed out, "G-Mama tried to stand up after the doctor left. He told her something awful. He told her she might not never walk. She tried to prove him wrong but he was right."

G-Mama brushed Erica's helping hand away. She turned over and proclaimed, "Well, I still say he ain't right!"

Oh, how good it felt to hear G-Mama sass. Adam

173

loved G-Mama, sass and all. "G-Mama, I'm glad you ain't dead."

"Dead? You're like that doctor. Expecting the worst. Face hanging long and said. I told him, 'Say it! Don't trim it up or polish it down, just say it.' I told him straightforwardness is the only way, and it is. Honesty and straightforwardness."

Erica picked her up and put her back on the bed. "How's that hip feel now? We got to listen to the doctor."

"Not when he ain't right, I don't have to. Why, right now is the prime of my life with a close family again. I ain't spending it laying down. I like the measure of my life to run full force, not in dribbles! I yearn for action."

Erica said, "Still, I think we better have the doctor see if you injured your hip again in this fall."

"Never fell. I felt the weakness and *eased* down. I ain't lost my senses. But that's just the first of my tries. I'll do a little practicing in bed before I try it again though. Little Adam, I want you to make the footboard of the bed solid so's I got something to push against."

"I will, G-Mama. I'm sure glad you ain't dead. I sure think you can walk again if you try. But right now, I sure got something important I come home to tell."

"You mean it wasn't G-Mama you brought me home to see?" Erica asked.

"Nope. I brought you home to ask you a question. You want to adopt me and Eva?"

Eva and G-Mama both gasped, and G-Mama scolded. "The nerve of you, Little Adam! Now that's a fast way to wear out your welcome!"

Adam ignored the sass. He wanted to tell what he'd found out with the best of words, words fitting the occasion. "What's a judge's *chamber*?" No one answered. They just stared at him dumbly. Well, he didn't mean to embarrass anyone by showing up their ignorance of a word. But as long as they weren't sure enough of its meaning to answer, he was on equal footing and could use it. "Well, I went into the judge's *chamber* in the spare room in back of Lonny's store, and he says it ain't against the law for a single woman to adopt if she is a rare exception. You are a rare exception, Erica Wheeler, and I'm going to prove it to him. You got a steady job, and you got someone home to take care of us, and we can help out if we need to. Just give me some biscuits and a Clabber Girl baking powder can filled with beans and I could pick a fair amount of cotton."

"Whoa!" said Erica Wheeler. She stood amazed and exuberant. "Judge Nagle is a fair man. But expecting him to be persuaded easy is like expecting a chicken to sell its own eggs. We better get our case perfected and down in writing. He's got a real eye for any legal loophole. Get me the tablet, Eva."

Eva ran for some paper and Adam searched out a

pen, but the point was broken and he had to search some more.

He'd just found a good one and was passing it along to Eva when Erica's voice came out sort of shameful, saying, "I'm sorry, G-Mama, no one has asked your opinion."

"Don't talk soft to me. Don't be afraid of wounding my feelings, Ericky. I don't wound easily. But look here, I got my own home and these are my own *God*-given grandkids. Ericky, I don't know what's in your head or how Little Adam happens to be in on it, but . . . Look, ain't it enough in one day to have that doctor lowering his word of doom, without you pointing up the fact that I'm a crippled old lady laid up in someone else's house, unfit to care for my grandkids?"

G-Mama's eyes were sizzling mad, and her jaws tight and old. But Erica started talking soft again, and the mad and tightness smoothed out.

"Dear G-Mama, I didn't mean to ever . . ." Erica began and was holding her hand.

Eva interrupted. "G-Mama, you ain't got enough sense to blow up a paper bag either! Nobody's pointing at you!"

"Eva Braggs, I'll tan your fanny!"

Adam pushed G-Mama a little so she settled back down and away from his sister. "G-Mama, you cain't win against every law. Erica Wheeler knows the law inside and out, and she loves the law and she . . .

loves us too . . . I think." He was getting so bold in some things that it frightened him. He was afraid to look towards Erica. Anyway he better finish what he had to say to G-Mama. "It seems we got to look up to two women, and I'm of the opinion that Erica Wheeler ought to be the one that's telling us how to deal with the law, since that's her business and all. Why, she was walking the rounds with her daddy when . . ."

Erica said, "Little Adam, save that until some other time. Thanks for the tablet, Eva. Now first . . . Why, what's this?"

Eva said, "While Little Adam was rattling on, I figured I'd best start my part of the adoption. I'm done."

Erica Wheeler kept her eyes on the words Eva had written and said in a voice that almost sounded as if she were crying, "This ain't exactly what I had in mind but it's perfect, Eva." She cleared her throat and said, "Now G-Mama, nobody has said you cain't choose your own way. But try to realize there are some things too late to be decided on. You already busted your hip, the kids already came and found you a sick woman, they do need a proper home, you cain't get to first base if you plan on arguing *that* with Judge Nagle.

"These are things that have been decided for you. Now let's pick up on the things you can decide on. You know you are as welcome here as the day is long.

177

You know I kind of cotton to having an older woman in the house."

"I don't know nothing!"

Erica talked on in sort of a guarded way, same as G-Mama with her shouting. It was a delicate moment again. Erica said, "Out of the mouth of a child . . . and heart too. G-Mama, we're a couple of hard beat old women and we better take notice of these children, take a few chances on love, open up a bit. Now listen to me and let's get our papers ready."

G-Mama laid back and relaxed of her own accord this time. "I'll thank you to shut up a minute, Ericky, and let me have my moment to think. Not the children nor you has lived as long as me. I figure I know enough about living and dying. I don't need to be seeking advice. Life just pours out its experiences upon a person, and there you be just taking it all in. But there does indeed come a time of selecting what you'll keep, I reckon."

Adam said, "That's right. Eva and me's had experiences too. And I select to leave no legal loopholes. I select that we be adopted legal, don't we select that, Eva? Here, let me see what Eva wrote down."

G-Mama started talking again so Adam had to wait before Erica would let him read what Eva wrote. G-Mama said, "My boys lived with me for years without being adopted. I never forsook them once nor they me. I know it ain't the same with all people, though. I know Viv lived on her hurts and hate. Poor

178

soul, she was one that couldn't let go to caring, Ericky. I guess it weren't fair to Eva."

"Now you're thinking right, G-Mama. Eva sure does need real adopting. I wouldn't mind it being made legal on me, myself. Actually, I'm all for it," Adam agreed.

Erica said, "And I'm for it."

"I got my own place in the woods to think about too. You're asking an old woman to give up where she's served her man, raised her kids, knows the grounds and woods and all its herbs, has a choice bunch of livestock . . ."

Erica said, "From what I hear, Leatha and Mr. Jones will be happy to buy all your livestock if you'll wait until next fall for full payment. No one asks you to give up your home and the woods. These twins'll need someplace to go on weekends when their school chores are done. Soon as you feel up to riding in my truck, we'll take runs out there regular enough."

"I'm setting up, ain't I? I could ride in that truck right now. A couple them hogs, we'll kill and cure. I'll fry up the sausage or have Eva to."

Adam said, "We ain't going anywhere until we get our papers done and see that judge. Let me see what Eva wrote, Erica."

"Adam's right," said Eva.

"You're outnumbered," said Erica Wheeler, and she handed Adam the paper that Eva had written.

179

Well, now, if Eva hadn't written the doggonest thing that Adam had ever read! Boy, she sure was thinking like a twin, all right. It was exactly what he would have written himself, given the time.

fourteen

The sky was clear as new ice the next morning when they got up. Everyone had worked together to get Erica's case written out and rid it of errors.

The three of them marched straight into the judge's chambers in back of Lonny's store.

Adam said, "Judge, this is Sheriff Erica Wheeler and she's a strong woman. Our G-Mama's home with a busted hip, but she ain't exactly weak either. Anyway, they got me. I ain't a man yet, but I'm a twin, and that's about as good or even better. We're both from strong stock. My Uncle Windy was . . ."

Judge Nagle said, "Look, sonny, is this a brag session or did you come here on business? Howdy, Ericky."

"Howdy, Judge. Nice day, ain't it?" Erica was smiling. Fact was, she'd been smiling like that all the way over to see the judge. Well she might be, for it was a nice day, hanging full of the smell of roses. Even Scrawny had been wagging his tail and appreciating it all until he'd got left outside the door of the judge's chambers.

Right off, Judge Nagle seemed to punch down the niceness of the day. "Ericky, you out of your mind? It's you this boy's wanting to get adopted to? You planning on giving up your office as sheriff? You got just about as much need for kids as I got need for a third thumb."

"I don't know your needs, Judge, but mine are to have you hear me out, to sign my documents, and to perform your duties as a judge and let me give these kids a legal home."

Any fool could see that the judge was filled with curiosity up to here the way he looked at Adam and then Eva. "Twins, you say?"

"Yep! I weighed more than Eva but we was born on the same day. Maybe we don't look alike and maybe we don't act alike, but we understand each other a whole lot. It's almost like understanding yourself, and that don't always agree neither, you know. I guess what I mean to say is that Eva thinks soft sometimes and so do I at times. Other times Eva can think just as solid and . . . like there's a girl-part to my thinking and a boy-part to hers and, well . . ."

"Like in all of us, son. Go ahead."

"Well, I just wanted you to understand that it was

Eva, a girl, who thought our document up, but I might have thought it up myself, given the time. Come on, Eva, let's read it to the judge."

The judge's chambers got real quiet as Adam read along with his sister, Eva:

"We promise to take this woman, Erica Wheeler, as our legal mother, and G-Mama as our legal grandmother, to honor and obey, to cherish and love till death do us part."

Judge Nagle said, "Well, I'll be blast! Okay, Ericky, let me read what your case has to say, and then we'll consider signing adoption papers."

"We've already signed it. It's legal," Adam said. The judge got a strange kind of look on his face and sat very quiet. Erica didn't say anything either. Adam was afraid that maybe he was thinking up a legal loophole. So he grabbed a pen off the judge's desk and wrote right there in the little space next to *obey* the words *and help*. "We ain't babies. We can help out a lot." The judge seemed to take proper notice of what he'd done and the words he'd said.

Erica said, "Okay, rascal. But if you'd left it stand just as it was, between me and G-Mama, we'd have seen to it that you helped." She gave his hair a fine messing up and went on to hand the judge her papers.

The judge read them and when he finally put them down in front of him, he slapped his hands flat on the table and said, "Now ain't all of this a pistol? Initial

183

your addition here, Adam. Okay, Ericky, you can sign the papers soon as I call some witnesses."

The witnesses came and it was done. Adam said, "You heard the judge; he took the *Little* off my name. I'm Adam now."

Judge Nagle declared loudly, "So be it! I now pronounce the whole kit and kaboodle of you *a family!*"

Then there was a lot of laughing and backslapping. Adam wasn't laughing to keep from crying, he was laughing because he was laughing. Just like there'd be times to cry when he needed to cry.

Erica had her arm around Eva. She looked to Adam and said, "Hi, son."

Adam said, "When I signed that part about obeying, that just meant doing things around the house."

Erica said, "I'll give the matter lengthy thought, Adam. But right now we got to hurry back to tell G-Mama. This is no time to leave her wondering and waiting."

They started to leave but the judge called after them, "Ericky, sure you ain't left anyone out? What about that howling pup outside the door?"

Adam answered, "Oh, you mean Scrawny? He's took the law in his own hands long time ago and got adopted without no help from a judge."

BERNIECE RABE drew from her own experience in writing *The Orphans*. She depicts a way of life very real to those who lived in the small towns of southeastern Missouri during the 1930s. Referring to Erica Wheeler, Mrs. Rabe says, "When I was a child, we had a woman sheriff. I didn't think it was unusual —just assumed all towns had them. And my son's mother-in-law was adopted by a single woman in the 1930s. That *was* unusual, but she found the legal loophole that allowed it."

Mrs. Rabe observed a difference in the way men and women handled the strains imposed by the Depression. "I watched men laugh away hard times. They had to, in order to withstand the tremendous burden of providing. I wanted to show how men repressed the hard times—Uncle Burl with brandy, Uncle Windy with storytelling, and Little Adam by big talk.

"The women tended to let their unhappiness surface. I think they were better off. For all, fight was a sign of life and survival. I wanted to show women who fought—spunky G-Mama, tough Erica, realistic but scared little Eva." As evident in *The Orphans*, Mrs. Rabe believes "hard times create their own kind of humor."

A former model and teacher, Berniece Rabe lives in Sleepy Hollow, Illinois. She recently received the Golden Kite Award of the Society of Children's Book Writers for *The Girl Who Had No Name*.